Easter Eggs, Broken Beds, and Murder

Noella Lee

Chapter One

I hate being volunteered for something I don't want to do. It's one thing if I willingly volunteer for something, but it's another thing if someone else volunteers me for something. Time is too precious for people to take it away from you. Whether I spend it doing something productive or lying on the couch, counting the cracks in the ceiling, that's my prerogative. You don't have the right to choose how I spend my Fridays.

I blew out a breath and stretched my neck, trying to alleviate the pain. Turning my head to look at Mama, I asked, "Why are we here again?"

"Because I took that corner around the aisle in the grocery store too fast and damn near threw out my hip when I was trying to get away from Jan," Mama said in a low voice. "She caught me when I was hobbling and forced me into this. Now be quiet and put another Snicker in that egg."

Mama tore open the wrapping of a mini Snicker and popped it into her mouth.

"How did she even convince you to come?" I asked, grabbing a brightly-colored egg from the table and pulling it open. "You don't let anyone convince you to do something you don't want to do."

Mama shrugged. "She brought the Lord into it. What was I supposed to do? She had me, and she knew it."

I sighed again and opened another bag of candy. "I understand you being here, but why am I here?" I complained.

"Because if I have to suffer, then you have to suffer," Mama said, ripping open a Kit-Kat and taking a bite. She put a hand on her hip and shook her head in annoyance.

I shook my head and looked around the room. We were in the church's back room, surrounded by other women who were standing or sitting at tables that were mini workstations. Some of the women made baskets filled with colorful paper grass, toys, books, and knick-knacks. Others had bags of candy in front of them and were busy filling colorful eggs with candy for the church's big Easter egg hunt on Sunday. There was a feeling of excitement in the air as women talked and laughed. Someone had brought a speaker, and old-school R&B music played in the background. There were a couple of babies in strollers, sleeping or staring at us; a few toddlers were playing in the corner, unaware that the toys they were playing with would be put back in the Easter baskets, and they would think they were brand new on Sunday.

Mmm, I don't know about you, but the holidays were a big deal in my small town. And no holiday was bigger than Easter Sunday. There was something special about Easter. It was like the best of every holiday wrapped up into one day. Yes, it was a time for us to worship and remember what Jesus did for us, but it was a holiday that fell during great weather, there was lots of food, candy and toys, and most of all, and I mean most of all, it was time to show out with outfits. Ohhhh, come on, somebody.

You don't understand. This was the time to show up and show out. This was the time to dazzle the other church members with your outfit, never mind that you see those same people every Sunday. And yes, you dress nice every Sunday, but this was the day you had shopped for. You went from store to store looking for that perfect outfit, and if you are a woman of a particular age, the perfect church hat. This was the day that you found *that* outfit to hurt *everybody's* feelings when you walked in. Ohhh, and I can't wait to see it. (I'm not really sure that vanity goes with the day you are trying to celebrate Jesus's sacrifice, but hey, it somehow works.)

"Ah, ah, ah, Maven. I saw that," Jan Campbell said, wagging a finger as she walked over to our table. She was in her early forties with dark brown hair, caramel-colored skin, and subtle makeup. Jan was wearing a blue dress over a white turtle neck top, and the fluorescent lighting in the room kept twinkling off the small diamond earrings that adorned her ears.

"Excuse me?" Mama said, looking at Jan. She was not amused.

"This candy is for the children," Jan said, placing a delicate hand on one of the bags. "Not for eating."

She pulled back, and a little laugh came out of her mouth. "We wouldn't want the children to be without candy on Easter, now would we?" she asked in a sickly sweet voice.

"Yeah, because I can eat over twenty bags of candy, huh, Jan?" Mama asked sarcastically.

Jan waved a hand at her. "Well, Maven, I didn't mean anything by it, honey. It's just that Reverend Montgomery wants the Easter egg hunt to go over without a hitch, and as one of the chairwomen for this year's festivities, I want to make sure that everything goes smoothly."

Jan looked Mama up and down and then leaned in to whisper, "Plus, don't you think you've eaten enough candy in your life? I didn't want to say anything, but I noticed that your pants have gotten a little tighter over these past few Sundays."

Mama stared at Jan. "Jan, you're lucky we're in the house of the Lord, and there's a peanut stuck in my tooth, and I'm in desperate need of a toothpick."

Jan pulled back. "What is that supposed to mean— Oh, no, no! Darlene, that's much too much grass for that basket, sweetheart!"

We watched as Jan walked off to bother a woman at another table.

"Do you think she practices that southern accent, or does it come naturally?" I asked, looking as Jan directed Darlene on the proper way to fill a basket with grass.

"It's fake," Mama said in a flat voice. "We're from the same town. Why is she the only one that sounds like that? Huh? Tell me that?"

Mama held up her hands and blew out a breath. "Let's hurry up and finish these eggs because if I have to deal with her, I'm gonna mess around and miss heaven."

Mama and I continued working on the eggs for the next two hours. Finally, we were done and put them in a big box. I turned around and grabbed my purse from a table as Mama grabbed the empty candy bags and threw them into a large black trash bag. Jan came by our table and looked at our work.

"Oh, good! You're all done," she said, beaming at us.

"Yep," Mama said, picking up a few empty candy wrappers. "Those eggs are filled and ready to go. Bless the little babies' hearts. They'll be excited about their eggs."

"Good, good. So, what time should I expect you tomorrow to hide the eggs?" Jan asked.

Mama paused in picking up trash from the table, and I froze in the middle of pulling my black shirt down around my hips. I slowly lifted my head and stared at Jan.

Mama blinked several times and shook her head to clear it. She straightened and let out a little chuckle. "Ohhh! Oh, Lord. My bad! Whew!" Mama said.

She turned, looked at me, and laughed, making a little motion with her hand. I started doing an awkward laugh, and Mama turned back to Jan. (Oh, no. Jan's not laughing.)

"Ohh, I must have misheard you," Mama said. "I'm sorry. I thought you said you would see me tomorrow to hide these eggs. This big box of eggs that's sitting right here on this table. This box here."

"I did," Jan said, smiling. Mama and I instantly sobered.

Mama dropped the trash bag. "What are you talking about? My job is done! I volunteered to stuff eggs, and I did that!"

"But we need someone to hide the eggs, Maven! How do you think the eggs will get hidden for the children?!" Jan asked.

"I don't know, and I don't care," Mama said. "I don't have small children. This whole thing doesn't matter to me."

"Maven, you don't mean that," Jan said. "Think about how happy the children will be. Cookie?"

"Don't look at me," I said, folding my arms. "I didn't want to be here in the first place."

Jan turned back to Mama. "Maven—"

"Jan," Mama said, leaning on the table. "It is Good Friday. You've taken my whole afternoon when I was planning on eating a good plate of fried catfish, crawfish etouffee, and potato salad and resting my feet at home. But I came here because you caught me when my hip gave out—"

"What?" Jan asked, confused.

"—and if you think that you are going to take my Saturday, too, then you are gladly mistaken. I will not be here. Don't look for me. Don't count on me. Don't call me," Mama said in a firm voice.

*****

"Don't look for me. Don't count on me. Don't call me, huh?" I said, looking around the large grassy field.

"Cookie," Mama warned. "Now ain't the time. Don't make me give you Jan's tell off."

I looked at her. "I'll risk it because it's been two days, and you have yet to tell her anything. I don't think you're going to say anything to her. I think you might have met your match, Mama. There is someone who is a better manipulator than Maven Simmons."

"Hush your mouth," Mama said, and she gave a fake shudder. "That day will never come."

"Mmm," I said, not commenting and looking around. It was a beautiful day. The sun was shining down brightly on us, but a breeze in the air made it comfortable and not overbearingly hot. A good amount of people were already here hiding Easter eggs, their hands full of grocery bags that held the candy-filled treats.

"Let's go find Jan and get this over with," Mama said, reaching down to lift the hem of her blue floral maxi dress. She gingerly stepped down from the church's back steps, her gold sandals sinking into the grass, and started searching for Jan.

We nodded our heads to several people in greeting, stopped to talk to a couple of friends, and laughed with a few others about the fact that we were out here on a Saturday doing this when we could be home, resting for tomorrow. It took us a while to find Jan, who was tucked away under a large white tent that sat almost at the back of the church's property. She lounged in a chair, dressed in a green tank top, white shorts, a visor, and sunglasses covering most of her face. Next to her was a table that held several boxes filled with Easter eggs. Netta Dixon stood at the table, refilling people's grocery bags and sending them off with instructions.

"Oh, you have got to be kidding me," Mama murmured. (I couldn't see her eyes because she was wearing sunglasses, but I'm pretty sure she had rolled them.)

"Are you irritated because Netta is at the table or because Jan is sitting there and fanning herself like she's a queen overseeing her hive?" I asked in a low voice.

Netta Dixon and Mama had gone to school together and had never been friends. There was just something about those two that caused them not to get along. Even helping Netta out in the past hadn't caused them to move past their feelings for each other. They soon slipped back into their regular routine of ignoring each other or being sickly sweet.

"A little bit of both," Mama said. "You ready?"

"Always," I said with a nod of my head.

"Hey, y'all!" Mama said in a loud voice, smiling big. She waved a hand at Netta and Jan as we walked toward them. "Mornin'!"

"Mornin'!" Jan said, smiling and waving at Mama. "I'm glad y'all could finally make it! I thought y'all might have forgotten where the church was!" She laughed. "Y'all were taking so long!"

"Hmmm," Mama said, struggling to keep the smile on her face. "Well, we're here now, and I see you're busy at work, so Cookie and I are here to help you with your heavy workload! The Lord knows we wouldn't want you to break one of your fingernails before church tomorrow. What would people think?"

"Mmmm," Jan said, smiling and continuing to fan herself. "Well, I'm just glad that I had Netta here to help me. You know, Maven, some of us are called to serve the Lord, and some of us need a little push to get through that gate, but the point is that we all get through, huh?"

Mama opened her mouth to speak, but I quickly opened my mouth to cut her off. (Once people start bringing the Lord into it to throw insults, I get nervous. I don't know if He is amused or mad, and the way my life is going, I can't afford to be on His bad side.)

"So, were we supposed to bring our own bags, or do y'all provide the bags?" I asked loudly and then tried to smile when they looked at me.

"I have bags here for everyone," Netta said, reaching down and pulling out two bags. She shook them out and started filling them with eggs. "Everybody has already done most of the work, but you two can still help out. We need these eggs hidden by that back fence over there. Try not to put them near the trees. We don't want kids going too far from the church."

Netta handed the bags to Mama and raised a brow. "You think you can handle that?"

Mama stared at her and then slowly took the bags. She made a motion toward her face.

"I'm glad to see you went to the doctor and got that fixed," Mama said.

Netta frowned. "Got what fixed?"

"Oops! Nevermind. Come on, Cookie," Mama said, putting an arm around my shoulder and pulling me away from the table. The outraged voices of Netta and Jan sounded behind us.

"Mama, that was petty," I said, shrugging her arm off me and reaching up to fix my hair.

"Yeah, well, sometimes pettiness has its place," Mama said. She held out a bag to me. "Here, take this."

I grabbed it, and we walked to the area we were supposed to cover and started hiding eggs. Cautiously bending down, I placed an egg halfway underneath a bush, letting it peek out slightly so a child could easily find it. Mama paused and looked at me.

"Is there a reason you're moving like that?" she asked.

"Moving like what?" I asked, moving my shoulders to put my hair behind me without actually touching it.

"Moving like that," Mama said. "What's wrong with you? Did you hurt your back or something?"

"I'm trying not to mess up my hair," I said. "Do you know how long it took me to wash, dry, and flat iron it last night? I'm trying not to mess it up before tomorrow. You know I never straighten my hair."

"Hmmm," Mama said. She placed a hand on my chin and moved my head to get a better look at my hair. "I did mean to tell you this morning that you had done a good job on your hair. It looks good."

"Thank you," I said, beaming at her. Coming from Mama, who was one of the best hairdressers to ever live, that was a high compliment.

"I could have done it for you," Mama said. "Or better yet, I could have done a sew-in. They have good hair textures now. I could have found one that would have looked like your hair blown out."

"I know, but I didn't want to bother you," I said. "Plus, there's something about seeing your own hair."

Mama smirked. "You wanted to see how long your hair was."

"That, too," I admitted. "But now I'm struggling. I'm afraid to move too much, or I'll start sweating from my scalp, and all those hours last night were pointless."

Mama shook her head. "That's a damn shame."

She reached into her bag, pulled out an egg, opened it, and took out the candy. Putting the egg back together, she dropped it in the bag and tore open the candy.

"Really? Isn't that for the kids?" I asked. "You're going to let some kid open an empty egg on Easter?"

She waved a hand. "They'll be fine," she said. "Their parents need to teach them that not everything you come across in life is going to be a prize, and tomorrow might just be the day for them to learn that lesson."

"Hey, Maven!" a woman said in a loud voice.

Mama turned her head, and a smile spread across her face. She lifted a hand and waved. A woman in her early fifties with warm brown skin and medium-length hair, wearing a pair of sunglasses, walked toward us. She had little weight to her, and her curves were shown off in her denim shorts and black tank top.

"Well, if it isn't Ms. Angelique Sullivan," Mama said, leaning in for a hug. "How are you doing, sweetie? Hmm, it's been too long."

"Yes, it has," Angelique said, stepping back from their hug. "It's not the same since you retired. I miss talking to you at my appointment every two weeks."

"It's not like I've moved out of town. You can still find me," Mama said. "You should come by the agency, and we can sit down and have a long talk. Catch up on everything."

"I need to. There is so much I have to tell you," Angelique said.

"Uh-uh, I don't like the sound of that," Mama said. She lowered her voice. "Your oldest still giving you trouble?"

Angelique rocked back on her flip-flops and stuffed her hands into her pockets. "Well, you know how it is. She's in that phase where she thinks she's grown."

"Mm-hmm," Mama said, nodding her head.

"And now she done got herself a little boyfriend, and they claim they're in love," Angelique said.

"Oh, Lord," Mama said. She looked at me. "Cookie, here. Take this bag. Angelique, you remember my youngest, Cookie."

"Hi," I said, raising a hand in greeting.

"Hi," Angelique said, nodding her head. "How you doin' sweetie? Oh, Maven, she's so pretty! She looks just like you!"

"Mm-hmm," Mama said, smiling. "Cookie, go hide these eggs while I talk to Angelique."

"Got it," I said.

I walked away and tried to look around for another spot to hide an egg. A few more eggs went under some bushes, and I placed a few on a bench. I sighed and stopped to look around. It seemed like all the good spots had been taken. I had wandered around so long that I found myself at the back of the church again.

"I'm trying to work, Faith," a man said, irritation in his voice.

"I'm not asking for much. I'm just asking where you stand," a woman said.

My ears perked up, and I casually walked closer to the church's back door. It was opened a crack, and it seemed like whoever was talking didn't realize that the public could hear their business.

"We've already talked about this," he said. I jumped when the sound of something heavy hit the floor with a clank. "I'm not ready to get married."

"But—"

"Faith," he said, a bite in his voice. "I don't want to talk about this anymore. I've got to get things ready for tomorrow, and I only have so much time."

There was silence for a few moments, and then the woman finally said, "Fine."

The door opened, and I jumped and turned away. I reached into my bag and threw an egg on the ground. I looked back and gave the woman a weak smile and a "Hey!" She looked embarrassed and quickly walked down the steps and towards the left of the church, disappearing out of sight.

I blew out a breath and walked back to Mama and Angelique, who had moved on from family issues to Angelique's problems at her job. Mama glanced at me and turned her head to fully concentrate on me.

"You haven't hidden those eggs yet?" she asked. "What's taking you so long?"

"I don't know where to put them," I said. "Everywhere is taken."

"Hmm," Mama said. "That's good enough. Put them in the car. We'll take them home."

"I don't blame you," Angelique said. "I don't know why Jan made so many eggs. Each child is going take home thirty eggs at this point!"

Mama looked at her. "You never told me how she roped you into this," she said.

"She caught me last night at the nail salon," Angelique said. "My nails were drying, and I couldn't escape her."

"Sounds like Jan," Mama said, nodding her head. She looked at me. "Are you looking for someone?"

I felt my cheeks heat at being caught.

"More like trying to avoid someone," I said. "I may have been caught eavesdropping on someone's conversation."

"Oh, was it good?" Mama asked.

"Mama," I said, rolling my eyes. "I'm not going to repeat what I heard. That would be wrong."

"Mm-hmm, spill it," Mama said.

"Mama—"

"I will mist the top of your head in your sleep."

"So, I was by the church's back door," I said, pointing to the building. "And I heard a man and a woman speaking, and it sounded like she was asking about marriage, and he was adamant that they were not getting married."

Angelique frowned. "Did you see who it was?" she asked.

I shook my head. "No, but he said he had to get things done around the church, and it sounded like she was getting on his damn nerves," I said.

"Things done around the church?" Angelique said. "Ohhh, you know who that sounds like? Faith Sanders and William Turner."

"William Turner and Faith Sanders?" I said. "I know them. They were seniors when I was a sophomore in high school. That didn't look like Faith."

"Well, you haven't seen her since you left town, and four kids will do that to you," Mama said.

"Four kids?!" I said. "They got four kids?!"

"Mm-hmm," Angelique said. "They've been together since they were sixteen. It's been thirteen years and four kids, and he has yet to marry that girl."

"Hmmm, it's a damn shame," Mama said as she crossed her arms. "Putting all those babies on that girl and won't marry her."

"Wait a minute now," I said, holding up a hand. "It's not about a man having the choice to marry a woman. Maybe they've been happy for the last thirteen years and didn't need marriage. Y'all are placing all the power in his hands. What about her?"

"Cookie," Mama said, looking at me. "Any man who sits around and puts four babies on you but claims he's not ready for marriage is playin' games with you. A man who wants to be with you will be with you and make it very clear."

"Mm-hmm," Angelique said, nodding her head. "And that girl has been playing house since she was eighteen. You don't play at being a wife if you don't want to be a wife. That girl is just a placeholder."

"A placeholder!" I said.

"Mm-hmm," Angelique said. "Mark my words. The minute he finds something he likes, he's gonna dump Faith and marry his new thang in two weeks."

"And leave her ass with four kids," Mama said, rolling her eyes.

"Okay, clearly, there is a generational difference here. I'm going to let it go because I can see that I'm going to lose," I said.

"I'm glad that you're aware," Mama said.

"Angelique!" a man shouted.

Angelique turned her head and raised her hand to a tall, heavyset black man with a bald head. She turned back to Mama.

"Girl, I gotta go. That's my husband. I told him we would be here thirty minutes tops, and we've been here for over two hours, and I still have to go to the store to get my ham for tomorrow," she said.

"Ohh, you better go," Mama said. "They're probably all gone by now."

"I know," Angelique said. She started walking away and turned back to yell, "I'm going to come by the agency one day, and we'll talk!"

"Okay. You have my number!" Mama said.

I lifted the bags in my hands. "Where do you want to hide these eggs?"

"I told you the car," Mama said. "I'm not dealing with Jan anymore. These kids will be fine."

"So, we're leaving?" I asked slowly.

"Yes, but not in an obvious way," Mama said. "Let's just make our way to the church and then get out of here."

"I'm with it," I said, and we started to slowly walk towards the church. "Hiding eggs is not fun. Why do I remember Easter egg hunting as fun?"

"Because you were finding them as a kid," Mama said. "It's fun finding them, not hiding them. Lord, I remember letting you children actually dye real eggs and then hiding them for y'all to find."

"Oh, yeah," I said, smiling at the memory from when I was six. "That was fun."

"No, it was stank," Mama said. "We couldn't find one of the eggs. It took three weeks and my house smelling like your Uncle Willis for us to find that damn egg. I vowed never again."

"I don't know," I said. "I would do it for my future children. Maybe you just needed a little map of where you put everything."

"Hmmm," Mama said. She paused as we reached the front of the church and grabbed my arm. "Isn't that William Turner right there?"

I looked at the parking lot and squinted. William was standing between two cars and seemed to be arguing with some guy. It appeared to be pretty heated between the two of them because William turned away, and the man grabbed his shoulder, and William turned around and pushed him. Hard.

"Ohhh," Mama and I said at the same time.

"I hope they don't get into a fight," I said, frowning in concern.

"I kinda hope they do," Mama said. "I haven't seen a good fight in ages."

"Mama!" I said in shock.

"I'm just joking, honey," Mama said, patting me lightly on the arm. (No, she's not.) "And look, it's over anyway. They stopped fighting."

I turned back to see William and the man walking away from each other, but you could still feel the anger coming off both of them. The man got into a truck and backed out of a parking spot while William walked to the church and stopped in his tracks when he saw us.

"Uh, hi, Ms. Maven," he said and came towards us.

"Hi, William," Mama said with a big smile on her face. "You remember my daughter Cookie, right? I think y'all went to school together."

I raised a hand and waved. "Hello. I think I was a few grades behind you."

William nodded to me and then stuffed his hands into his jean pockets. "Um, I hope that you didn't see—"

"That big fight you had with a man between those two cars?" Mama asked. "Oh, no, honey. I didn't see it."

William dropped his head and then looked at Mama. "I'm sorry about that," he said. "It was nothing."

"Looked like something," Mama said.

"It was really nothing," William assured us. "It was just a misunderstanding."

"Well, hopefully, you don't have any more misunderstandings," Mama said. "How's the new job going? I understand that Pastor Montgemory hired you as the church's new handyman?"

"Yes," he said. "It's going well, ma'am. I've started my own company, and I'm a maintenance man for several buildings around town."

"Oh, really?" Mama said. "Do you have a business card?"

"Yes," he said, reaching into his pocket. He pulled out his wallet and handed Mama a business card.

She took it and looked at it. "Hmmm, Turner's Handyman Services," she said. Mama looked at him. "I'll have to keep you in mind. I've been thinking about getting someone to come by and do a few things around the office."

"Give me a call," William said. "I'm reasonably priced. If y'all will excuse me, I have to get back to the church and finish the things the pastor wanted. Y'all have a nice day."

"You, too," Mama said.

We watched as he went into the church and then looked at each other.

"Hmmm," Mama said, raising a brow.

"Mm-hmmm," I said, turning with her and walking to the car.

Chapter Two

"Get away from the darn pan, boy!" Mama shouted.

Marques jumped and dropped the knife he was using to cut a slice of ham. It hit the kitchen floor, and he cursed.

"Don't curse on the Lord's day, Marques," Mama said as she fixed the sleeve on her light green jacket that matched her dress.

"Sorry, it kind of just slipped out," he said, grabbing a napkin to clean up the mess. He threw the knife in the sink and stood up. Smiling, he said, "Aww, you look nice, Mama."

Mama turned around and did a pose. "Do I, though?"

"Mama, you know you look good," I said, looking at my makeup for the last time in my compact mirror. I closed it and looked at her. "It took you a month to find that dress."

"And it was worth every dollar," Mama said, beaming. "And now for the final piece."

Mama picked up a light green hat and walked to the mirror hanging on the wall. She looked at herself and carefully placed the hat on her head.

"Perfect," she said, stepping back.

"Uh-oh," I said, smiling. "Not the hat."

"You don't know how long I have been waiting for this day," Mama said. "I can finally be one of those older ladies who wear church hats."

Mama paused and stood straight. "Oh, Lord! I'm finally old enough to be one of those older ladies who wear church hats!"

"I don't get it," James said from the couch. He was dressed except for his suit jacket, which was thrown over the arm of the couch. "Can't you wear a hat anytime to church?"

"Technically, yes," Mama said, walking to the kitchen counter and leaning a hand on it. "But there was something special about those *big* church hats the older ladies would wear when I was growing up. Every week they would come with a different one and it would match their outfits. It was like there was an unspoken rule that you had to be a woman of a particular age to wear those hats."

She walked back to the mirror and looked at herself. "And as a little girl, I vowed that I was going to be that woman one day. I couldn't wait." Mama looked at me. "Now, I wish I could go back in time, hit myself upside the head, and break that freakin' clock."

I laughed and pulled down the hem of my lavender-colored dress. "When is Ren coming? We're gonna be late for church!"

"He's coming," Mama said, walking to the kitchen and fixing the foil on the pan that held her ham with the special glaze. "He stopped to pick up Alexandra."

"Oh! Alexandra's coming?" Marques asked, fixing the band that held his long dreadlocks. "That's a big step. Bringing your girlfriend to church for Easter Sunday?"

"And for dinner with the family," Mama said with a smirk.

"Dang," Marques said, shaking his head. "All I know is that as his brothers, James and I are in charge of his bachelor party."

James looked surprised and then smiled.

"Please," I said and rolled my eyes. "James can't get into any of the places you're thinking of, Marques."

"I know somebody who can make him a fake id," Marques said.

"Marques!" Mama snapped.

"I'm joking, Mama," he said. He put his arm around her shoulders. "You know I wouldn't do anything to get the boy in trouble."

He leaned back and mouthed to James, "I got you!"

Mama's head snapped to him. "I saw that," she said, holding up a finger, fire in her eyes.

"What?!" Marques said innocently. "I didn't do anything!"

"I saw you, Marques Simmons!" Mama said.

"Mama, I didn't do nothin'," Marques said, holding up his hands and laughing.

I shook my head and walked to the door as Marques continued to protest his innocence.

"Hey, y'all! Happy Easter!" Ren said with a big smile on his face. He leaned down and kissed me on the cheek.

"Hey!" I said, smiling. "Hey, Alexandra!"

"Hi, Cookie," Alexandra said. She looked stunning this Sunday. Her closely cropped hair looked like she had gotten a fresh cut, and she was wearing a light blue dress with a subtle amount of cleavage that matched my brother's tie. Sapphire earrings decorated her ears.

Ren frowned. "What are they arguing about?" he asked, pointing to Mama and Marques.

I glanced back. Marques was still laughing, and Mama was now gently hitting him with a dish towel.

"You'll understand someday," I said and closed the door. "They're here! Are we ready to go? I want to get a good seat!"

"Please," Marques said, walking out of the kitchen. "You want to show your hair off."

"That too," I said. I smiled. "It's down to the middle of my back."

Marques and Ren groaned and rolled their eyes.

"You don't understand hair trouble, Marques!" I yelled. "With your unusually long locs! Get away from me!"

"If y'all don't stop yellin'," Mama said, grabbing her purse. "I have been up since four, cooking food so that all I have to do is reheat it when we come back. I'm already tired before my day has even started. I don't feel like hearing yellin'!"

"Sorry, Mama," Ren, Marques, and I mumbled. (How does your mother reduce you to a child that quickly?)

"Good," Mama said. "Now, let's talk about this car situation."

"Let's take two cars," Marques said. "We're not gonna fit into one."

"One of y'all can ride with Alexandra and me," Ren offered. "I'm blocking y'all in anyway."

"Hmmm," Mama said. She turned and looked at James. "James, why don't you go with them? This would be a good time for you to ask Ren for help with your math class."

James opened his mouth.

Mama looked at Ren. "He needs help with his math class," she said. "A B- is not acceptable in this house."

Ren laughed and hooked his arm around James's shoulders. "Come on," he said. "We'll figure out what days of the week I can tutor you."

They walked out the door as I slipped on my matching jacket and grabbed my purse.

"All right. Let's do this!" I said.

The church was packed full by the time we got there. Some people were sitting in the pews, talking to each other, waiting for the service to start, and others were standing in the aisles chatting and laughing. Men and women were dressed in every color possible and were in their finest with new shoes, dresses, shirts, suits, and skirts. Hair was freshly cut, dyed, freshly pressed, and curled. If you looked closely, you could find multiple women with puffy, red eyes hidden under concealer from the long hours of trying to get themselves and their families ready for this day. However, I must say, every hour of frustration, looking for the perfect outfit, moving funds around to pay for it, and feeling unappreciated was worth it. We were a fine-looking group of people.

Pastor Montgomery came out of a side door, and the deacons followed, cueing that people should take their seats. He smiled at the congregation and opened his bible.

"Good morning, church," he said in a booming voice.

"Good morning," we said back.

"I said, good morning, church," he said louder.

"Good morning," we yelled, laughing.

"All right," he said. "I was getting worried there for a minute. On this blessed Sunday morning, let us remember the sacrifice that our Lord and Savior Jesus Christ made for us. One that He did not have to make, but one that He gladly made for us sinners."

"Amen," several voices said, and people clapped.

"Please turn to…"

So was the beginning of a three-hour service. Between the several songs the choir sang and Pastor Montegomery's preaching, we were there for a while.

Don't get me wrong. It was a good sermon, and I enjoyed it. It was just long. Very long. (But would it really be church if it wasn't long? I mean, we went through a lot Monday through Saturday. You better thank God you made it to see Sunday.)

"Amen! Amen!" Pastor Montgomery shouted as he clapped, sweat pouring down his face. He wiped it with a towel. "Oh, Amen! Whew!"

People were standing, waving their hands. Some eyes were closed, their mouths silently moving as they prayed.

"Uh," he said, looking up to his congregation. "The service may be over, but you don't have to go home."

"We are grateful to the wonderful committee which has put on the Easter celebration after church," he said, looking towards Netta, Jan, and several other ladies who nodded their heads at the congregation. "From my understanding, there will be refreshments and an Easter egg hunt for the little ones. I hope you can stay and join us."

With that, church was over. I felt a tap on my shoulder, and I turned around to one of my best friends.

"Hey, are you and your family leaving right now?" Angie asked.

"We were planning to. Why?" I asked.

"Could you help me out with Sky?" Angie asked, glancing down at her daughter, whose head was full of curls. "My mom sprained her wrist, and I would feel more comfortable having someone with me for the Easter egg hunt."

"Sure, no problem," I said. I tapped Mama on the arm and told her the problem.

"Oh, sure, no problem, honey," Mama said to Angie. She looked at Sky and smiled. "Are you excited for the Easter egg hunt, sweetie?"

Sky smiled and bounced up and down. "Yeah! I'm gonna get a lot!"

"Absolutely," I said. "Especially when you have your mom and me on your team. Let's go!"

It took a while, but we finally made it through the crowd and to the back of the church. Angie went to a table to get an Easter basket while I stood with Sky and our families. Several families stood with their kids, waiting for the event to begin. Other members from the church had moved to the various tables that had lemonade and cookies and got refreshments. They were staying to watch and just have a good time.

"Here you go, sweetie," Angie said, handing Sky the basket.

"Thank you," Sky said, her eyes big as she looked over the grass, trying to spot eggs.

"All right, everyone," Jan yelled, clasping her hands together in excitement. "On the count of three, the Easter egg hunt will begin! One! Two! Oh!"

Before she could even get to three, several children took off, which caused other children to run, too, for fear that all the good eggs would be taken. (You can't do nothin' with bad kids!)

"Oh, no, you don't!" I said, bending down and snatching an egg before a kid could take it.

He frowned at me. "Aren't you too old to be out here?" he asked.

"Aren't you too old to have an Iron Man undershirt?" I asked. "What are you, fourteen? Get out of here, kid, before I make my older brother jack you for your basket! Scat!"

I walked to Angie and Sky and threw the egg into Sky's basket.

"Did you have to do that?" Angie asked, pointing a hand at the kid who was walking away in a huff.

I looked at Sky. "Your momma's nice. I'm not."

"I like it. It's getting me eggs," Sky said and then took off, her little legs flying across the grass.

"Sky—!" Angie called out in concern. "Jesus, she runs fast! Come on!"

We took off after her. For a seven-year-old, Sky was ruthless when it came to gathering eggs. She dodged, slid, jumped, and snuck around other children like an expert. Soon her basket was overburdened with eggs, and Angie had to carry it.

"I think— Oop," Angie said, catching an egg before it hit the grass. She plopped it back in the basket. "I think it's time to call it quits, Sky."

"Just a few more," Sky said, her eyes scanning the grass.

"Sky," Angie said with that mother's warning in her voice. "You have enough eggs. In fact, I think you've taken all the eggs they had out here."

"Mmm, Jan made sure there was a lot," I said, looking around at all the kids in the area. I leaned in close and covered my mouth. "Although, I did see Sky sneak a few eggs out of other kids' baskets. I wasn't going to say anything, but you know."

"Sky!" Angie said in disbelief.

Sky looked up at me and frowned. "I don't like you," she said.

I shrugged. "You'll grow out of it when you're sixteen, and you need me to lie to your mom," I said.

Angie looked at me. "You're not going to lie for my kid," she said.

I laughed. "Of course not!" I said. "I won't be that type of aunt!" (Of course, I would.)

"Cookie," Angie said, stopping and turning to me. She held up a finger. "I swear if I find out that you cover for Sky when she becomes a teen, I'll—"

"You'll what? You have nothing to threaten me with, Angie."

Angie's eyes narrowed. "I'll tell your Mama about the time we were fifteen," she said.

"Oh, you dirty heffa!" I hissed. I looked around and then stepped closer to her. "We *vowed* to never speak of that day again! Never!"

"You left me no choice!" Angie whispered. "I have to protect Sky!"

"I was just playing about Sky!" I whispered. (No, I wasn't.) "But you didn't have to bring up when we were fifteen! You know what? That's why nobody likes you!"

Angie gasped.

"Ohhh, I found a lot of eggs," Sky said.

"See, that's what caused that day to happen when we were fifteen," Angie said, sticking her bony finger into my chest. "That attitude right there! Did you listen to Caroline or me? No! You thought you knew better, and look what happened!"

"Can you lower your voice?!" I said, looking around. I fixed my jacket. "I have a reputation around here."

"One egg, two eggs, three eggs…" Sky counted.

"What reputation? A reputation of destruction and deviancy?" Angie asked.

I looked at her and then slowly started to nod my head. "Alright, Angie. Alright," I said, holding up my hand. "Cute. You got me. Zing."

Angie smirked.

I ran a hand down my dress to smooth out an invisible wrinkle. "And that is why God allowed that track in the back of yo' head to show for the last half hour!"

Angie gasped, and her hand went to her hair while I turned away from her with a snap. Suddenly Sky screamed, fear streaking through her voice. I turned around while Angie dropped the basket of eggs. They fell to the ground and scattered as we ran towards the trees.

"Sky!" Angie screamed.

"Sky!" I yelled.

People stopped and looked. Several men started running towards us to see what was going on. Angie and I burst through the trees and spotted Sky. She stood there in her little yellow Easter dress, eggs sprinkled around her feet. Her eyes were huge as she stared at the ground in shock, and her breath came in short pants.

"Sky!" Angie said and grabbed her, pulling her close to her chest. "Oh, my God, sweetie! What's wrong—? Oh, my God!"

Angie stood up and jerked herself and Sky back.

"What?" I asked, shaking my head in confusion and stepping forward. "Oh, no."

Laying on the ground was a black man wearing a dark grey suit. He was lying on his stomach, his face hidden by the bushes, but his shoulder-length dreads tied back in a low ponytail were peeking out from underneath the leaves. The back of his skull looked bloody, and a wrench was lying next to him with blood and hair stuck to it. I swallowed, feeling a wave of nausea go through my stomach. I placed a hand on it and tried to calm my nerves.

"What's going on?" a man asked, coming through the trees. Several people had finally caught up with us and looked at us for answers. They were concerned that something had happened and wanted to know if they needed to fight, search, or pray.

I sighed and said, "Somebody royally messed up Easter."

Chapter Three

"Okay, everybody, get away from the body," I said, turning around and waving my hands at the group. "We have to call the police and preserve the crime scene. Yada, yada, yada."

"Who put you in charge?" a guy asked, frowning at me.

"Who better to be in charge? Who has more experience with dead bodies?" I said. "Raise your hand."

I put my hand up smugly. My smile dropped, and I looked at Fred Johnson.

"Well, that's not my problem. You have a curse over your family. You need to go see someone about that," I said. "The point is that we need to get away from this body and call the police! Go!"

I shooed them with my hands. We walked out of the trees, and people immediately started asking questions, and of course, somebody had to say that we had found a body. People were shocked and started whispering among themselves, wondering who it was.

"I need to get back to my parents," Angie said, still in shock. "Sky is probably traumatized. I need to make sure she's okay."

"Mm-hmm," I said. I looked at Sky and bent down. "How are you feeling, honey?"

"I lost my eggs," Sky said. Then something dawned on her. She looked up at her mom. "Where's my basket?"

"Huh?" Angie asked, shaking her head. "What?"

"My Easter basket of eggs," Sky said. She looked between Angie and me. "Where is it?"

"Oh! Um." Angie looked around. "I must have dropped them when I heard you scream."

"*You dropped my eggs!*" Sky said in disbelief. Tears started to well in her eyes. "I worked so hard for them!"

"Sky—" Angie started.

"And we found them," Mama said, walking towards us with my brothers and Alexandra. She held out the basket to Angie. "Here you go, honey. I told your parents to wait for you at the front so that y'all can get out of here in a hurry. I'll let the police know to go by y'all's house."

"Thanks," Angie said gratefully. She grabbed Sky's hand, and they disappeared into the crowd.

I stood up and asked, "How did you know that was Sky's basket?"

"I didn't," Mama said. "When all the commotion started, I figured we should come and see what was going on, and I saw the basket on the ground. I scooped up the eggs and thought I would find who the basket belonged to or at least turn it back in at one of the tables."

"Sooo, you gave Sky a basket full of eggs that could have potentially been another child's basket?" I asked. "What if another kid started crying?"

"Then I would have suggested that we walk out of here fast but at a pace that didn't raise suspicion," Mama said. She nodded her head at the trees. "What happened?"

I sighed and folded my arms. "Sky took off when Angie and I weren't paying attention, and she wandered into the trees. She found a dead body."

"A dead body?" Marques said in disbelief. He frowned. "Who?"

"William Turner," I said.

"William Turner!" my family said as one, shock appearing on their faces.

I nodded my head. "His skull was bashed in with a wrench, but I still recognized him."

"I remember William Turner," Ren said, fixing his tie. "He and Faith were tight in high school."

"And still are from what I heard," Marques said. "I don't think they ever broke up."

"No, they didn't," Mama said. "They have four kids."

"Four kids?" Ren said. "Whew, Lord! That is a lot of kids."

Alexandra eyed him, and Ren smiled, giving her hand a quick, tight squeeze as he winked at her.

"And he didn't marry her," Mama said.

"Well, Mama…" Marques started.

Mama slowly turned her head towards him.

"…that is a shame and a disgrace and something I would never do!" Marques said, shaking his head. "Uh-uh, you don't have to worry about me. I would never do that!"

Mama turned back to me.

"Good save, Marques," I said, nodding my head. "Real smooth."

"Stop it, you two," Mama said, waving a hand. Her mouth was turned down, and her brows were furrowed. "This is serious. Does anybody remember seeing him during service?"

We all shook our heads.

"I wasn't paying attention," I said. "He wasn't on my mind."

"I haven't seen him since high school," Ren said. "Well, you know, I see him in town every once in a while, but I haven't *talked* to him since high school."

"Same," Marques said, nodding his head.

"Hmmm," Mama said. "He's working for the church now, and I'm sure he came to service."

"He was dressed in a suit," I said. "I'm positive he must have attended."

"Hmm," Mama said and started looking around. "That means Faith probably attended, too. I wonder where she is?"

"*Nooo! Nooo! No!*" a woman screamed, and we all turned our heads.

We watched as Faith burst through the crowd and tried to run for the trees. Tears were streaking down her brown, round face, ruining her makeup. A couple of men grabbed her to stop her, and some women stepped in front of her to try to comfort her. I spotted four small children, ranging from eight to three, standing behind her, looking confused and scared.

I shook my head. "Well, there's your answer," I said.

"Wow, I feel so bad for her," Alexandra said, putting a hand to her chest. "I can't imagine."

"Hmmmm," Mama said, looking at the scene. The women pulled a sobbing Faith away and brought her to a tent.

"What?" James asked.

"Nothing," Mama said. "Nothing yet. Just a feeling."

"What feeling?" I asked.

"Just a feeling," Mama said, glancing at me.

"I'm your business partner. Shouldn't you let me know about this feeling?" I asked.

"Not yet," Mama said.

The sound of sirens in the distance made people tense, more from the feeling of disbelief that this was actually happening and that we would be stuck here for a long time than from anything else.

"Let's go find a seat while we can," Mama said, turning towards the church. "We don't want to be standing for this."

*****

"How much longer are they going to be?" Marques asked, shifting on the pew and fixing his jacket.

"A lot of people showed up today," Mama said as she fanned herself with one of the church's programs. "They need to talk to everybody."

"It's been over three hours," Marques complained. "I have ham to eat. Can't we go to the station later and give our statements?"

"People forget things," I said, stretching my back. "The police want them while they're fresh and can remember things."

"Mmm," Marques said and put his arm on the back of the pew. We sat quietly as officers walked around and talked to people.

"I don't want to cause any trouble, but is there a reason that woman is eyeing us?" Alexandra whispered.

"Who?" I whispered back.

"Her," Alexandra said, subtly nodding her head toward a few pews ahead of us.

"She's talking about Jan," Mama said in a loud voice, not caring who heard us. "Jan has been eyeing me for the last half hour. I don't know what her problem is. She's over there eyeing me like I'm the one causing trouble in her house, but that's her husband. She needs to take that up with him."

Jan gasped in outrage.

"Mama, please," I begged. "I know it's hot. I know they cut off the air conditioning. I know. But please…"

"If you must know," Jan said, standing up despite her husband trying to grab her arm and stop her. She walked over to us. "I was thinking that this was your fault."

Mama stopped fanning herself. "My fault?"

"Yes," Jan said.

"My fault?" Mama repeated.

"So you have bad taste in hats and bad hearing," Jan said.

(Well, this Easter was nice while it lasted. I mean, despite the dead body, it was good. I got to wear my new dress and show off my hair. The egg hunt was fun until you know…the body. And I got to—)

Mama slowly stood up and looked at her. People started whispering and turning in their pews, excitement in their eyes that a fight was about to happen—nothing like being a first-hand witness to a tell-off.

Mama slowly lowered her hands and clasped them in front of herself. "Jan, please tell me, how is this *my* fault?"

"Well, this church has never had a problem before you. It has been a pillar of the community, and suddenly three dead bodies in less then a year and all have a connection to you," Jan said.

The whispering got loud, and people nodded their heads.

"I don't know how you drew that conclusion, but I'm going to let it slide because, just like your fake accent, I know you like to live in a make-believe world," Mama said.

One woman snickered and then covered her mouth, trying to hide her laughter.

"Everything was going fine until that *one* found a body," Jan said, pointing at me.

I raised a brow.

"That *one* has a name, and what would you have liked, Jan?" Mama asked. "For his corpse to rot in the woods while we continued with your horrible and boring-ass Easter egg hunt?"

Jan's mouth dropped. "My Easter egg hunt was fabulous!"

"It was trash!" Mama snapped. "Y'all didn't even have enough decency to get the good bakery cookies. Y'all got the cheap ninety-nine-cent cookies and put that on a plate."

Mama huffed and fixed her jacket. "And had the nerve to buy that sweet behind punch that is too thick and try to water it down to make it stretch! If you need money, say that!"

"You know what, Maven Simmons—"

"Oh, I've never backed down from a fight!" Mama said, moving into a stance.

"Woah, woah, woah!" Shay said, waving his arms. Pastor Montgomery was behind him and looked concerned.

I looked up at him in surprise. He was dressed in jeans, black and white sneakers, and a graphic t-shirt that said something about science. Stubble was across his jaw, and it looked like he hadn't shaved in a day or two. (I liked what I saw.)

"I don't know what's going on, but ladies, please stop," Shay said, holding out his hands.

"She—!" Jan started.

"The gentleman asked you to sit down, Jan," Pastor Montgomery said in a firm voice, giving her a look. She huffed, and her husband gently pulled her back to the pew they were sitting on. He looked around the church. "I know this is a difficult time, and I'm sorry that it is taking up your Sunday, especially this Sunday. But please just bear a little longer, and we will all be able to go home."

Pastor Montgomery looked at Shay. "Soon?"

Shay hesitated and then nodded his head. "I'll try my best," he said.

"Good," Pastor Montgomery said and then turned around and walked through the church doors.

Shay sighed and looked around the church. Turning to us, he asked, "You're the one who found the body?"

"Technically, yes," I said.

"Of course you did," Shay muttered.

"Hey!" I said, frowning.

"Why don't y'all come outside, and we can talk?" he suggested. "Maybe let the tension ease from the air a little bit."

"Okay," Mama said, bending down to grab her purse. She looked at Jan. "But she knows where to find me."

Jan stiffened in her seat but didn't turn around.

"Did you have to?" I asked as we walked out of the church.

"Yes," Mama said. "Because Jan's anger is misplaced. She's mad that her event went wrong and needs somebody to let her anger out on."

Mama looked at me. "Don't let people use you as a punching bag, Cookie. People need to learn how to deal with their emotions and not take them out on others. Maybe I looked like a fool in there, but I also let people know that I won't stand for any kind of mistreatment. Big or small."

I nodded my head and shrugged. "I guess."

Looking at Shay, I said, "From the way you're dressed, I'm guessing you weren't at church today?"

(I knew he wasn't at church. I had looked for him, but you can't let a man know that you're looking for him.)

"No," Shay said, flipping through his notebook. "My Aunt Cherry wasn't feeling well, so we decided to skip church."

"Oh, no," Mama said. "I'll stop by later and drop off a couple of plates of food."

Shay shook his head. "I got it," he said, looking up. "I cooked."

We all paused and looked at him.

"What?" Shay asked, looking offended. "I can cook!"

"Hmmm," I said. "You just don't look the type."

"I have to agree," Mama said. "You look like the type to put several prepackaged foods in the oven and then put them on a plate and think you did something."

"I can cook!" Shay said. "It's not fancy, but I can follow instructions. I made a ham, rolls, mashed potatoes, and green beans."

"Hmm, were the mashed potatoes from scratch?" I asked.

"A box, but—"

"See?!" I said, holding out a hand toward him while I looked at Mama. (I use boxed potatoes too, but that's not the point.) "I knew it."

"Did you snap the green beans yourself?" Mama asked. (I've never seen Mama use nothin' but canned green beans, but once again, that's not the point.)

"Who snaps green beans anymore? Ms. Maven, when was the last time you saw someone snap a green—" Shay started to ask. He shook his head to clear it and held up a hand. "Can we talk about the case?"

"So, you're the lead detective, huh?" Mama asked, moving her purse to the crook of her arm.

"Yeah," Shay said. "It was supposed to go to another detective, but something happened, and he had to back out, so it fell to me."

"Hmmm," Mama and I said at the same time as we looked at him.

"What?" Shay asked, looking at us.

"Nothing," Mama and I said at the same time.

Shay's eyes narrowed, and he looked between us.

"Let me handle this case," he said. "You are *not* on it. I repeat, you are *not* on it."

"Of course not," Mama and I said at the same time.

*****

"Okay, let's list the things we know so far about the case," Mama said. "James, get that whiteboard out of my bedroom."

"Do I heat the oven to three-fifty or four hundred for the ham?" Marques asked from the kitchen.

Mama waved a hand at him in annoyance. "We can eat later, Marques. We need to focus on the case."

"*Eat later!*" Marques said in disbelief. "Why can't we eat now and not mind our business?"

I pulled off my jacket and threw it on the couch while James set up the whiteboard. Grabbing a marker, I uncapped it and started writing.

"William started working for the church..." I looked at Mama.

"About three weeks ago," Mama said.

"Three weeks ago," I said, writing on the board. "And we know that he started his own company, and he said that he worked for multiple businesses around town."

"Mm-hmm," Mama said, folding her arms. "And he was in a relationship with Faith and had four kids."

"And things weren't going well with Faith from what I heard," I said. "She wanted marriage, and he didn't."

"And he got into a fight with a mystery man yesterday in the parking lot," Mama said.

"What happened?" Ren asked. I told him about the incident we saw with William and the man. "Did you see this guy at church?" he asked.

I shook my head. "I don't think so," I said. "But I can't be sure. It was unusually packed, even for an Easter Sunday."

"I don't think so," Mama said. "He didn't look familiar to me. I don't think he's from around here."

I nodded my head and turned to the board. "We also know that he was murdered today. We just have to pin down what time exactly."

Mama nodded her head. "He was dressed in a suit."

"And the murder weapon was a wrench," I said, frowning. "But there was no toolbox around."

"And didn't you say something about Easter eggs?" Mama asked.

"Yeah," I said with a nod. "They were all around his legs when we got to his body. That's how Sky found him."

"That's strange," Mama said, shaking her head. "From what I remember, all the eggs were hidden. Why would he have a bunch of eggs around him? What was he doing with them?"

"I don't know," I said. "William's kids were there. Maybe he left the service a bit early and took a bunch of them to give to his kids."

"It's something you would do, Mama," Ren said from the kitchen as he stole one of the rolls.

"That's true," she said. Mama turned to the group. "Okay, this is how we're going to do it—"

"Wait," Marques said, looking up from the oven. He held up a hand. "Are you trying to *include us* in this?"

Ren shook his head. "I came for the Lord and food, not murder."

Mama closed her eyes for patience. She opened them and blew out a breath. "If *everyone* helps, we can solve this *faster*," she said slowly. "Understand?"

"I understand that in thirty to forty-five minutes, this ham is going to be done," Marques said, closing the oven. He shook his head. "Sorry, Mama, but I remember the last time. I'm not helping anymore."

"Do you not remember that someone almost burned down your garage?" Ren asked.

"I almost got arrested because of you," Marques said. "Never again."

"That was your fault," Mama said, pointing a finger at him. "I appreciate the love, but I told you to calm down, and the insurance company fixed my garage. Now, listen you two, this is what we do. We solve mysteries."

"No, that is what you two do," Marques said, pointing a finger between Mama and me. "I'm going to solve the mystery of how many plates I can eat in one day before I have to unbuckle my belt."

"I can't believe I lost my figure for you—*Will you stop eating the damn rolls, Ren?!*" Mama yelled, causing him to jump. She rolled her eyes. "Good Lord, the things aren't even heated! Save some for the rest of us!"

"I'm hungry!" Ren said, putting the foil back over them.

Mama sighed and closed her eyes. Taking a moment to calm down, she opened them and looked at me. I shrugged.

"It's up to you," I said. "What do you want to do?"

"Fine," Mama said. "Then it will just be James, Alexandra, Cookie, and me."

"Alexandra?!" Ren said. He shook his head and looked at his girlfriend sitting at the kitchen table. "You don't have to do this."

"Uh…" Alexandra said, her mouth open and her eyes wide.

"Yes, she does," Mama said, slowly walking over to her. She placed a hand on Alexandra's shoulder and smiled at her. "It will be good for us to spend some time together. I look forward to getting to know my daughter-in-law. Ain't that right, daughter-in-law?"

(Ahhh, Mama was dirty for that. Ren hadn't said anything about him and Alexandra getting married officially. We all could see that it was heading that way, but they had only been dating for a few months, and it was too soon to have discussions like that. Mama knew saying something like that was putting pressure on Alexandra and dangling a carrot in front of her.)

"I guess…" Alexandra said in an unsure voice as she looked at Mama. She looked at Ren. "I have helped before."

"I. Can't. Believe. You," Ren said, staring at Mama. "How low will you go?"

"To the very floor," Mama said as she walked to the oven and grabbed a set of red oven mitts with little lips printed all over them. "There are no guarantees in life, so you have to play every card you got."

"No, no, no," Marques said in a panic. "What are you doing with my ham?!"

"First of all, it's my ham," Mama said, taking it out of the oven and closing the door with her hip. "And it would be rude to go to a person's home without a little somethin'."

"*A ham?!*" Ren and Marques said at the same time in disbelief.

"Mama, you are just being petty now," Marques said. "You are not going to really travel with a whole ham. Come on, now."

"Mm-hmm," Mama said, the pan clutched in her hands as she walked to the door. "Come on, Alexandra! James, grab my purse!"

"I would like to say that this whole thing is ridiculous, and I don't like being a part of this family," I said.

"No one cares, Cookie," Marques said, leaning on the counter, his jaw tight.

"I know, but I just wanted it on the record," I said.

"Cookie, grab a towel so I can put this ham on my lap in the car. It's hot!" Mama yelled from the front lawn.

"You know what makes me sad," I said as I walked to the linen closet to get a towel. "This isn't the most ignorant thing I've seen in this neighborhood."

"It really isn't," Ren said, nodding his head.

"Cookie!" Mama yelled.

"Coming!" I yelled, grabbing the towel and closing the door.

"This is the last holiday I'm spending with you people," Marques said, rubbing his eyes in frustration. "So I hope y'all remember it fondly."

"Ohhh, I'm telling it to my children someday," I said, glee in my voice as I grabbed my purse from the couch. "Don't you worry!"

Rushing out the door, I pulled the front door closed and walked down the few steps to the front lawn. Mama was already seated in the backseat of the car. She held the pan slightly in the air so it didn't touch her thighs and burn her. Alexandra sat next to her, looking a little shocked that she was going with us, and James sat in the front, looking unbothered. (He was used to us by now.)

"Here," I said, folding the towel. I placed it on her lap, and she set the pan down. "Where are we going?"

"Faith's house," Mama said.

"Faith's house?" I said in surprise. "This soon? Her man just died a few hours ago. Isn't it too soon to go and talk to her?"

Mama shook her head. "Normally, I would say yes, but it happened at church. That means every woman is going to converge on her by tonight to try and comfort her. You know this town doesn't have anything going on. A good murder is like the Superbowl going into overtime. Get in the car."

"Okay," I said, shrugging and closing her door.

I hurried around the car and got in. As I started the car, Mama gave Alexandra instructions on whom to call to find out where Faith lived. I drove around for a while before we got the right address. Making a u-turn, I drove to Faith and William's house. It was a nice four-bedroom house that was a bit older but still a good family home with a neat lawn and brown roof.

"This is it," I said, turning off the car.

"Alright," Mama said. "James, open my door. Remember, say loving words and let Cookie and me take the lead."

"Got it," Alexandra said, nodding her head.

James nodded his head and opened his door. He opened Mam's door, and she got out of the car, still holding the pan.

"Are you sure you want to be with my brother after this?" I whispered to Alexandra as Mama walked to the door.

Alexandra smiled and did a slight shrug. "Hey, there's never a boring day with him," she said. She looked at me. "That's good, right?"

"If you say so," I murmured. (Personally, if I saw a man with all this going on, I would have left. But that's just me.)

As we gathered in front of the door, Mama nodded her head at it.

"James, knock on the door," she instructed.

James gave a firm knock on the door, and it opened with a slight creak. We all stared at it.

"Okayyy, maybe it's nothing," Mama finally said, breaking the silence.

"Oh, because a door that opens by itself always bodes well," I said sarcastically. I turned to Alexandra. "How many movies have you seen that a door that opens by itself bodes well?"

"Not one," she said.

"James?" I asked, looking at him.

"I'm still waiting," he said.

"Thank you!" I said, throwing up my hands. "Can we go back to the car? Please?"

"No," Mama said. She blinked a couple of times and then shook her head. "No. Um, maybe a couple of women are already here."

"I don't hear anything," I said. "There's nothing but silence. Listen."

We shut our mouths and waited. Nothing.

"Hmmm," Mama said. She pushed open the door with her foot. "Faith? Honey?"

"Who the hell walks into danger?" I asked, pointing a hand at Mama. "This is clearly the setup for a horror movie, and yet she goes forward?"

"Cookie, hush," Mama snapped, frowning at me.

"Oh, don't you raise your voice at me," I said. "I think history has proven that I *will* leave you if the killer comes."

"Ohhhh," Mama huffed and turned back to the door. She pushed it fully open and stepped inside. "Faith? It's Maven Simmons."

Mama slowly walked forward. We followed into the house, warily looking around.

"Faith?" Mama called out softly.

Walking past the living room, we turned right and walked into the family room. Stopping behind a couch, we looked at the floor. Faith was on the floor in front of the patio windows. The front of her dress was covered in blood. She was over a man lying on the floor, clearly dead from all the blood that had spread across his chest and pooled around his body. Faith looked up at us, breathing hard, and with a knife clutched in her hand, she said, "It's not what you think."

We just stared at her with our mouths open.

Finally, Mama said, "Well, maybe Marques is going to get this ham after all."

I frowned and looked at her.

"Oh, you have got to be kidding me!" a man said from behind us.

I turned and saw Shay standing behind us with a look of disbelief on his face. I turned away and sighed. (Yep, this seemed to be the norm for us.)

Chapter Four

Shay slowly walked towards us, his gun raised in the air.

"Put the weapon down," he said to Faith in a strong voice.

"I—" Faith opened her mouth to speak.

"Put the weapon down now!" Shay said.

Faith swallowed, dropped the knife to the floor, and raised her hands in the air. She struggled to her knees, slowly rising to her feet.

Shay glanced at us and said, "Move!"

"Oop," Mama said, and we all rushed away from the couch, moving to a corner and crowding together.

Shay slowly walked around the couch, his gun trained on Faith.

"Put your hands behind your back!" he said.

She followed his instructions, and then Shay quickly holstered his gun and pulled out a pair of handcuffs. Cuffing Faith, he pulled out his phone and called for backup. Soon there was the sound of sirens and officers coming into the house to take over the scene.

We stood outside and watched as Faith was put in the back of a police car, tears streaming down her face. She looked out the window at us and then turned away, her head hanging down.

"Mmm," I said. "What do you think?"

"I don't know," Mama said. "This isn't good."

"You think she did it?" I asked.

"Of course she did it," James said. "She was over him with a knife."

"Maybe it was an accident?" Alexandra suggested. "A lot of men attack women. Maybe he came after her, and she was protecting herself."

"Hmmm," Mama said. She looked at me. "Did you notice what I noticed?"

"That he was the same man we saw arguing with William in the parking lot yesterday?" I said. "Yeah."

"Not good," Mama said. "Not good at all."

An officer walked up to us and said, "You know the deal. Split and give statements."

"Can I at least put this in the car?" Mama asked, lifting the pan. "It's heavy."

Shay walked over to me and nodded his head at the officer who stood in front of me.

"I'll take her statement," he said. The officer nodded her head and walked away.

Shay looked at me and said, "What the—?"

"I know," I said, holding up a hand. "You don't have to say it. What are you doing here?"

"What am I doing here?!" Shay said. He shook his head. "Faith wasn't at church. She left with her parents before the police came."

I frowned. "Where are her kids?" I asked, looking around. "I didn't see them."

"Her parents have them," he said. "I went to their house first because I thought she was there, but they dropped her off here. She said she wanted to be alone, and they thought it was best to keep the kids."

"So, how long was Faith here?" I wondered out loud, pointing a finger at the house. "She had to be here for over two hours."

"Who is asking who questions?" Shay asked. He looked behind his shoulders and turned back to me. Pointing a thumb over his shoulder, he asked in a low voice, "And why is your Mama walking around with a pan that smells like ham?"

"Long story, and my family is very petty," I said. "Back to Faith. Any idea who the guy on the floor is?"

"No. Now back to questioning you," he said. "Why are y'all here?"

"We were doing the neighborly thing and coming to see how Faith was doing," I said. "I mean, her man just died. I felt for her."

Shay stared at me.

(Darn it, he knew me too well. I'm going to have to learn better acting skills.)

"Okay, we were coming to question her," I said.

"And…?" Shay asked.

"And what?" I said.

"You're holding something back," he said.

"Okay…maybe the guy on the floor is the one we saw William arguing with yesterday," I said.

Shay's eyes widened, and he pointed a thumb at the house. "That's the same guy?!" he said."

"Yeah," I said slowly.

"That's a big deal, Cookie. You should have led with that," Shay said.

"I was going to get to it eventually," I said, my eyes turning away from his. I looked at him. "What's going to happen to Faith?"

"I caught her in the middle of a murder. What do you think is going to happen?" Shay asked.

"Mmmm, I don't think she did it," I said.

"What makes you say that?" Shay asked.

I told him everything that had happened.

"The door was open when we got here," I said. "If she had been here for over two hours, why was the door open?"

"Mmmm," Shay said. The corners of his mouth turned down as he thought. He looked at me. "Maybe."

"I would just like to inform you that Faith Sanders is now our client," Mama declared, coming up behind Shay.

He looked at her. "Since when?"

She hesitated. "Since two minutes ago, but that is not the point," Mama said. "And as her investigators, we have the right to talk to our client. It's the law."

"There is no law that says that," Shay said.

"Yes, there is," Mama said.

"No, there isn't," Shay said.

"You know every law on the books?" Mama asked.

"Yes," Shay said, fed up with Mama. "Yes, I do. I know every law that was ever created, and there's no law that says investigators have the right to talk to their clients once they're arrested."

Mama stared at him.

"I know you're being sarcastic because you were pulled out of your bed on this blessed Sunday, but I swear, if I find a law on this planet that says investigators have the right to speak to their clients once they're arrested, I am rubbing it in your face for eternity," Mama said.

Shay nodded his head. "Noted. I look forward to that day," he said. He looked at me and whispered, "It will never happen. See you later, Cookie!"

Mama gasped as Shay walked away from us. She looked at me.

"I can't believe him!" she said.

"Let's just be happy that he let us go," I said. "He could have decided that we needed to go to the station to give our statements, and we could have been there all day."

"That's true," Mama said. She blew out a breath and put her hands on her hips. "I'm just upset about Faith."

"Are we really taking her on as a client?" I asked.

"Yes," Mama said, nodding her head. "I don't know if Faith did it or not, but she deserves someone on her side to hear her story, and I think we should be those someones."

*****

We walked through the front door, weary and disappointed that things hadn't gone like we wanted them to. Ren and Marques were sitting on the couch, watching tv. Their suit jackets were thrown over the arm of the couch. They looked at us and frowned, confusion on their faces.

"Dang, that was fast," Marques said.

Ren nodded his head in agreement. "I thought it would have taken y'all longer to speak to whoever y'all were going to speak to."

"Well, things didn't work like I wanted them to," Mama said, placing the pan on the kitchen counter.

"You brought the ham back?" Marques said, getting up from the couch and walking to the kitchen. He pulled back the foil and started picking at it. (Now, I know Mama is tired. She didn't even bother to stop him, and she was standing right next to him.)

"What happened?" Ren asked, looking at us.

"We went to see Faith," I said, pulling out a kitchen stool and sitting down. "And we found her over a dead man with a knife in her hand."

"Wait, this is death ham?!" Marques said, his mouth full. He gagged, went to the trash, and started spitting it out.

"Marques, stop that!" Mama fussed. "What's wrong with you?"

"Oh, my God, it was in my mouth," he said, gagging again and spitting into the trash.

"I swear this boy is big for nothin'," Mama said, shaking her head in annoyance as she leaned on the counter and tapped her fingers on it.

Marques stood up and wiped his mouth with the back of his hand.

"You're the one who brought back death ham!" Marques complained, pointing at the pan. "Do you know blood particles float in the air? They probably landed on the ham, and I put it in my *mouth!*"

"Where did you hear that, Marques? Where did you hear blood particles float in the air?" Mama asked in an irritated voice.

"From the internet, and don't you dismiss it because you get half of your detective information from the internet and tv!" Marques growled.

Mama's jaw tightened, and she looked at me.

"Checkmate," I said.

"I can't believe you brought that back," Marques said in disgust. "You should have thrown it!"

"Marques, stop talking about the darn ham!" Ren said. He looked at Alexandra. "Are you okay?"

"Yeah," she said, nodding her head. "It's fine."

"I really wanted ham," Marques said.

"Marques!" Ren snapped.

"Nothin' wrong with that ham," Mama murmured, drying her hands with a paper towel. She threw it away and went to the oven to turn it on. "That ham is perfectly fine."

"What. Happened?" Ren asked, getting fed up.

"I told you what happened," I said. "Faith was over a dead body with a knife."

"We're gonna eat that ham," Mama murmured as she put multiple pans in the oven to warm.

Ren's mouth dropped, and his head turned around the room as he looked at us. He sighed and rubbed his hands down his face.

"I feel like I'm in an episode of the Twilight Zone," he said, his voice muffled by his hands. He looked at Alexandra. "And what makes me more upset is that you seem okay with all of this."

"Hey, she's been around this family for a while and hasn't run. You should have known that she was a little off," I said.

"Cookie!" Ren said.

"I'm joking," I said. (I'm not.) I looked at Alexandra. "I'm joking. You know you're great."

"Do you think Faith did it?" James asked, opening a can of soda and sitting down next to me on a stool.

"I don't think she did," Mama said.

"She didn't exactly deny it, Mama," I said. "She said it wasn't what it seems. That's not a denial that she just gutted a man."

"Hmmm," Mama said with a slight shake of her head. "Where were her kids?"

"Shay said that her kids are with her parents," I said. I indicated with my head for James to hand me a pack of peanuts. "She wanted to be alone."

"We need to figure out who the guy on the floor is," Mama said.

I nodded my head as I chewed. "And why he was arguing with William yesterday?"

"Wait, the dead guy is the same guy that William was arguing with?" Marques said, and he shook his head. "Yeah, she did it."

"She did not do it!" Mama said. "You don't know that!"

"Hmmm, I don't know," Alexandra said, shaking her head. "It doesn't look good."

"Let's just focus on helping the girl," Mama said.

"What do you want to do?" I asked.

"We need to see Faith and talk to her," Mama said. She sighed. "Let's eat and get a fresh start tomorrow. Alexandra, be here by eight. Cookie and I like to get an early start."

"Tomorrow?" Alexandra said, frowning. "I have to work."

Mama stared at her.

"But I can call in sick," Alexandra said weakly.

"Don't you back down from her," Ren whispered fiercely. Alexandra looked at him and slightly shook her head. He ignored her and looked at Mama. "Mama, Alexandra isn't—"

"Alexandra isn't what?" Mama asked in a firm tone, staring him down.

"Alexandra isn't…sure what type of breakfast sandwich you like," he said weakly. "She's going to bring y'all breakfast in the mornin'."

He turned to Alexandra and whispered, "I'm sorry. I'm the oldest and her favorite. I don't want to disappoint her."

"It's okay," Alexandra said, patting him on the leg.

"Food's ready!" Mama said, smiling.

*****

"We need to canvas the neighborhood," Mama said as we stood outside Faith and William's house the next morning.

"Canvas the neighborhood?" I said, looking at her from behind my sunglasses. "I'm not walking around here all day. It's too hot for all this."

"There has to be someone who saw something," Mama said, spreading her hands out to the houses surrounding us. "That man snuck into this house in broad daylight. Someone saw something."

"It's not a bad idea," Alexandra said. "I know my neighbors and I always look out for each other, and we notice if there's something off with each other's places."

"Exactly," Mama said, smiling at Alexandra. "Y'all take that side of the street, and I'll take this side. We'll call each other if we find out something."

Before I could open my mouth, Mama took off walking down the street for Faith's next door neighbor.

"Okay then," I said. I turned to Alexandra and pointed a hand. "After you."

We walked in the opposite direction from Mama to the house next door to Faith's. I knocked on the door, and we waited for someone to answer. A minute or two later, a man opened the door and looked at us.

"Good morning," I said, smiling. "My name is Beaulah Simmons, and I'm a private detective investigating the crime that happened next door. I was wondering if you noticed anything—"

"Are you the police?" he interrupted.

"No," I said, shaking my head. "We're not the police, but if we could just have a moment of your time…okay. He didn't have to slam the door in my face like that."

"Next house?" Alexandra asked, looking at me.

"Next house," I said, nodding my head.

The next several houses weren't successful either. People either brushed us off or hadn't seen anything because they were out with family and friends. I sighed when the latest door closed in my face and turned away to walk back to the sidewalk.

"I'm confused," I said. "If everyone was out on Easter, then who are the people that were actually home? Because it seems like no one in this whole state was actually home for Easter!"

"I was home for Easter."

"What the—?" I said, looking around me.

I looked down to see a small kid on a bicycle. I frowned, looked around, and then looked back down at the little girl. She had a cute brown face with big eyes. Her hair was in plaits with little barrettes at the end and was smashed down to her head because she had a pink helmet and pads that matched her pink bicycle.

"How old are you?" I asked. "And why is there no adult supervision around?"

"My house is there," she said, pointing to a house several houses down from where we stood. "I'm four."

Alexandra and I gasped.

"And your momma let you out by yourself?!" Alexandra said in disbelief.

"I'm four," she said with a stubborn look. "I can take care of myself."

I let out a weak laugh.

"Of course, you can, sweetie," I said. I turned to Alexandra and covered my mouth to whisper, "I'm calling the law."

Alexandra nodded her head.

"I was here on Easter," the little girl said again.

"You were?" I said, pulling out my phone. "Good for you! And did you enjoy your Easter, sweetheart?"

"Yes," she said, nodding her head. "I got a bike."

"Ohhh, and what a pretty bike," Alexandra said. "It's very nice!"

"It is," the girl said. She frowned. "The man almost hit it, but he said sorry."

"Is there a special division for trifflin' parents?" I murmured, scanning my phone.

"A man almost hit your bike?" Alexandra asked with concern.

"Mm-hmm," the girl said, nodding her head. "But he said sorry and then went in that house."

She pointed to a house.

"That house?" Alexandra asked. "The one with yellow tape on the door?"

"Mm-hmmm," the little girl said.

Alexandra grabbed my arm and looked at me with a stunned look.

"Cookie, I think she's talking about…" She looked down at the girl and then whispered, "You know who!"

I looked down at the kid.

"What's your name, sweetie?" I asked, bending down.

"Jordan," she replied.

"Jordan," I repeated, smiling. "What a pretty name! So, you say this man almost hit your bike and then went into that house?"

"Mm-hmm," she said.

"How did he almost hit your bike?" I asked.

"With his truck," Jordan said. "I was doing circles in the street."

(Yep, I'm calling the law.)

"But he said sorry," Jordan said. "And my momma said I'm not supposed to be in the street. I can only be on the sidewalk in front of my house."

(Still calling the law.)

"Can you remember what he looked like?" I asked.

"Tall," Jordan said. She squinted in thought. "Bald."

That sounded like our guy.

"Can you remember what he was driving?" I asked.

"A truck," Jordan said proudly. "My big brother plays with cars. There's a difference between a car and a truck."

"Yes, there is," I said, my smile widening. "And he was driving a truck?"

"Mm-hmm," she said. "A grey truck with letters on the side. I can't read words, but I can tell my letters."

"Do you remember the letters?" I asked.

"Maybe," she said in an unsure voice, losing all the confidence she had moments ago.

I showed her my phone.

"It's okay if you don't remember," I said. "Just point to the letters you do remember."

I looked at Alexandra. "Can you write them down?"

"Got it," Alexandra said, pulling out her phone.

For the next few minutes, Jordan, Alexandra, and I went over the different letters on my phone, and she picked some out.

"That's all I can remember," she said, disappointment on her face.

"That's great," I said, patting her on the shoulder. "You did a great job, Jordan. Thank you."

"Cookie," Alexandra said in a low voice. I stood up. "I think I figured out what it said on the side of the truck. I don't think it was an M, but two N's. I think it's Brenner's Tow Truck Company. Look! The company's owner is the same guy we saw on the floor."

"Are you sure?" I asked as I took the phone from her.

She gave me a look. "You don't forget something like that, Cookie. Trust me. His face is burned into my memory."

"Hmmm," I said, looking at his smiling picture. I quickly read the page. It boasted about the company being a family business for the last thirty years. "Gary Brenner."

I looked at Alexandra. "His business isn't that far from here."

"Mm-hmm," Alexandra said, nodding her head.

"Hey! What y'all doing?!" a woman shouted at us.

I looked up and rolled my eyes. "Oh, now you care about your child?" I muttered under my breath.

"Mmmm," Alexandra said, crossing her arms over her chest. She pursed her lips, a look of judgment coming over her face.

"We've been here for how long?" I murmured to Alexandra.

"Too long," she whispered.

"I could have been gone Lord knows where with her child," I whispered. "Mmmm. Hi! Are you Jordan's mom?! I'm so glad to meet you!"

I put a big smile on my face and started walking over to the woman. She was dressed in a jogger set, and her hair was wrapped in a towel. It looked like she had just washed it. (Ohhhh, I am judging her!)

"My name is Beulah Simmons, and this is my associate, Alexandra. We're from the Simmons Detective Agency, and we're investigating the unfortunate crime that happened next door. Jordan was telling us that she saw a man go into the house. Did you happen to see him?" I asked, smiling big.

"Jordan, I told you to stay in the front yard and not to speak to strangers!" she fussed.

"I'm sorry," Jordan said, dropping her head.

"Oh, don't blame Jordan," I said. "She has been great and was in the yard just like you said. I was the one who started talking to her and…Ohhh, girl! Your nails are so nice! Who does them?"

"What?" Jordan's mom said, looking at her nails. "I do."

"No way!" I said, putting my hands on my hips. "They look professional. Are you a nail artist?"

"No, I just like saving money," she said. "They charge too much these days."

"Girl, I completely understand," I said. "If I didn't have loyalty to the girl I go to, I would leave. Are you sure you don't do them?"

"Well, I do them on the side," she said. "And I charge way less."

"Give me your number," I said. "Maybe if you don't mind, I can come by and get mine done sometime. What's your name?"

"Janae," she said, taking my phone and putting in her number. We talked for a few minutes about nails and how much she charged.

"So, did you hear anything from that house?" I asked, nodding my head towards Faith's house.

Janae looked at it and shook her head. "No," she said. "I feel bad for Faith. I didn't know her that well, but Jordan would play with her kids in the afternoon sometimes. I was inside cooking dinner when I heard the sirens and came outside to see what happened."

"Mmmm. Did you see a truck outside?" I asked. "Or maybe a truck passing by in the neighborhood?"

"What kind of truck?" Janae asked, confused.

"A grey one," I said. "With writing on the side of it."

"No," Janae said, shaking her head again. "No grey truck like that."

"What about this guy?" Alexandra asked, showing Janae her phone. Janae squinted at the phone and looked at the picture of Gary.

"No," Janae said slowly. "Never seen him. He's cute, though."

"Mmmm," I said. "Well, thanks. And I will call you soon about those nails, okay?"

"Alright, I look forward to it," Janae said, smiling. "Jordan put your bike in the garage and get inside. Your grandma is going to be here soon to pick you up."

"Okay," Jordan said, running to do what her mom said.

As we walked away from the house, Alexandra glanced at me.

"Are you really going to call her?" she asked.

"Hell no," I scoffed. "But Mama taught me that a little sugar and the thought of putting money in your pocket will make any person talk. Plus, I wanted her to get off of Jordan's back. That little girl didn't do nothin' wrong."

I dialed Mama's number and waited for her to pick up.

"Hello?" she answered.

"Hey, we think we have something. How about you?" I asked.

"Thank goodness," Mama said. "I'll meet y'all back in front of Faith's house."

She hung up without a goodbye. Ten minutes later, Mama walked toward us, looking frustrated and hot.

She stopped in front of us and said, "People in this neighborhood are rude as hell."

"Agreed," I said. "But we found thee most adorable little girl who saw the man go into Faith's house."

"She did?" Mama said, her eyebrows raising. "Tell me more."

We told her everything Jordan said and how we had tracked down Gary Brenner.

"Ohhh, this is good," Mama said, looking at his picture. "This is really good."

She looked at us. "Let's go to the tow company," she said and took off for the car.

"What?! Wait!" I said and hurried off after her. "Why?"

"Why not?" Mama asked, opening her car door.

"We don't have anything to go on," Alexandra said, getting in the backseat.

"So? You think a case is solved because all the evidence is laid out in front of you?" Mama asked. "You have to pick up the little pieces you have and do something with them."

"I guess you have a point," I said, leaning back in my seat.

"Of course I do," Mama said. "Alexandra, find the directions to Brenner's Tow Truck Company."

Chapter Five

After looking up the directions, singing to several old-school songs, and talking about people's children, Mama, Alexandra, and I arrived at Brenner's Tow Truck Company. It was a mid-size building, and I saw several tow trucks through the open garage door. Men and women moved around the garage; a few worked on the trucks while others got ready to go out on calls. Carefully, Mama parked the car along the curb, and we got out.

"Hey, don't I know that car?" I asked, pointing to a dark-colored sedan that was a few spots in front of us.

"Do you?" Mama asked, glancing at it.

"I think so," I said. "I know I've seen it before."

"Hey, there's Shay," Alexandra said.

"What?" I said, my head turning to the garage.

Shay was walking out of the office and down the steps with a man who was dressed in a blue work uniform. A frustrated look was on Shay's face as he talked to the guy. They paused in front of a truck, and the guy turned to Shay, shook his head, and shrugged. Shay's jaw tightened, and he nodded his head. He thanked the man and then started to walk away. He paused when he saw us standing there.

"Oh, absolutely not," he said.

"Now, Shay—" Mama began to say.

"No," he said, holding up his hand to stop her as he walked to us. He stopped in front of us. "Turn around and go home."

"Now, you know we're not going to do that. Why must we play these games?" Mama asked.

"Ms. Maven, I don't want y'all interfering with this case," he said. "Just let it go."

"How can we let go?" Mama asked. "We're on Faith's legal team."

"You are not on Faith's legal team," Shay said, shaking his head. "I don't know where you got that from."

"Lawyers…detectives…it's basically the same thing," Mama said.

"It is definitely not the same thing," Shay said slowly. "Not only is the definition different, but the whole school process is different…."

"How'd you find this place?" I asked, interrupting him.

"I ID'd Gary Brenner," Shay answered.

"How?" Mama asked. "Fingerprints?"

"Eyewitnesses?" I asked.

"Face recognition? Dental impressions?" Mama asked.

"His driver's license in his wallet," Shay said. He pointed between us. "You two watch way too much tv."

"Well, that was disappointing," Mama said, looking at me. "I wanted something exciting."

"Now, you two answer something for me. How'd you find him?" Shay asked.

"An eyewitness in the neighborhood saw him go into the house, and we were able to track down his business," I said.

"Who?" Shay asked, his eyes narrowing. "We canvased the whole neighborhood, and no one saw him go into Faith's house."

"Obviously, you didn't talk to everyone," I said, a gleeful smile spreading across my face. (Sometimes, it felt good outsmarting Shay.) "Wow, looks like we're just a little bit better than you, huh?"

"Cookie, this is serious. Who did you talk to?" Shay demanded.

"Sorry! The law says we have the right to protect our sources," I said as I began to walk around him.

"Bye!" Mama said, giving him a little finger wave.

"That only applies to journalists! Why do y'all keep confusing people's rights?! Jesus!" Shay snapped and stormed away to his car.

"Okay," Mama whispered to us. "Let's see if we can have better luck than he did."

She walked to the garage with a smile on her face and waved. "Hi!" she said. "Are one of you the manager?"

The man Shay had talked to looked up from a clipboard he was holding. He had dark brown skin, a low-cut fade, and his beard and mustache were neatly trimmed. The man was around 5'10 with a nice muscular frame, but he had a certain air about him that said he wasn't the friendly type.

"Yeah, I'm the manager," he said, his attention returning to the clipboard in his hands. "Can I help you?"

"Yes," Mama said as we walked over to him. "I'm Maven Simmons from the Simmons Detective Agency. I was hoping that you could talk to me about Gary Brenner?"

He glanced up at us. "What about him?" he asked.

"When was the last time you saw him?" Mama asked.

"Saturday," he said, putting the clipboard down on a table next to him. He looked at us. "He came in to catch up on some paperwork, and then he left by eleven. Now, can you tell me why a detective is looking into Gary?"

(Well, I don't feel very welcomed. Do you?)

Mama cleared her throat and smoothed a hand over her clothes, taking a moment to regroup.

"We are helping our client," Mama said. She swallowed. "I don't know how to say this. I'm so sorry, but…."

He frowned, and his brows came down over his eyes. "Are you working for the woman who killed Gary?" he asked.

"You know Gary is dead?" Mama asked in surprise.

He scoffed and walked around Mama. "I'm the one who identified his body last night," he said. Walking to the stairs, he looked over his shoulder and said, "I'm his brother-in-law."

"Oh, oh, hold on now," Mama said, hurrying after him.

"What do you mean 'brother-in-law'?" Mama asked as we followed him up the stairs and into a small office.

"I'm married to his sister," he said, going behind a desk. He started moving papers around, and a frustrated look came over his face. "Why couldn't he put anything where it should be?" he muttered, shoving a stack of papers aside.

"Sooo…" I said. "Do you know why Gary would be at our client's house, Mr…? Mr…?"

"Allen," he said, glancing at me. "Allen Moore."

"Mr. Moore," I said, smiling. "I'm Beulah."

"Alexandra," Alexandra said with a small wave.

"I don't care," he said, still looking for whatever paper was important to him.

"Ouch, that hurt my feelings, but whatever," I said. "So, why was Gary at our client's house?"

Allen sighed and leaned on the desk, looking at me. "I don't know," he said. "Like I told the guy who just came here, I don't know why he was over there."

"Do you know Faith Sanders and William Turner?" Mama asked.

"Not really," Allen said, moving another stack of papers. "Where is it?"

Mama slammed a hand on the stack of papers in his hand and pushed it down on the desk. Allen looked up and opened his mouth to speak, but Mama cut him off.

"Listen, young man, I know you have a lot going on right now, but there is a young woman with four kids who is being accused of murder, and I truly believe that this young lady didn't do it. Unfortunately, the person who was murdered was your brother-in-law, and I would like to think that you would take the time to help us figure out who did this," she said. Mama gave him a slow smile. "Now, put the papers down and talk to us."

Allen sighed and dropped the stack. He sat down in a chair and slouched back in it.

"I've never met Faith or William," he said. "I know William was working on my wife's business, but I've never met him."

"He was—" I said. We looked at each other in shock. "William was working on your wife's business?"

"Yeah," he said. He sighed and shook his head. "Gary knew William from back in the day. William had fixed a couple of things for him, so when William said he was opening a handyman business, Gary decided that he would help him out."

"By recommending him to his sister?" Alexandra asked.

"Yes and no," Allen said. "Gary also has another business. It's a mobile car wash business, but Gary kept a small storefront where an assistant could keep track of all the bookings, and they could store the vans in the back. The AC broke down, and Gary decided to call William and ask him to come by and fix it."

"And obviously Gary liked William's work," Mama said.

"Yes, especially because William went around the place and fixed other stuff for free," Allen said. "My wife stopped by the business one day, and Gary introduced them. She was impressed with everything William had done around the place. Ashley had just opened a bed and breakfast and thought it would be a good idea to have a handyman she could trust, and with Gary vouching for William…" He shrugged.

"Your wife hired him," Mama finished.

"Yeah," Allen said.

"When was this?" I asked.

"About a month ago," Allen said.

"And it was going good?" Alexandra asked.

"At first, yes," Allen said. "From what my wife told me, he was great, but then he started cheating her."

"Cheating her how?" I asked, frowning.

"He started charging her more, saying that he had to fix the same things twice or even up to three times, that he needed to get special tools to fix stuff and it was going to cost more…" Allen blew out a breath and shook his head. "He was screwing her over."

"And you never met this guy?" Mama asked.

"No," Allen said. "I planned to. This week was the last straw, but things have been crazy for the last few months, and Gary and I have been working overtime to make sure that the business stays afloat. That's why he and

I were both pissed about this last scheme William had pulled on Ashley."

"What happened?" I asked.

"He claimed the entire air conditioning system needed to be replaced," Allen said with a look of disgust on his face.

"Ohhh, that's not good," I said.

"But it's April," Alexandra said. "It's still pretty cool."

"But summer is around the corner," Mama said. "And you know how hot it gets around here. Lord, I can't imagine being without an AC."

"Exactly," Allen said. "And Ashley is trying to make a cozy bed and breakfast with all the accommodations. Plus, her business is new. Can you imagine the reviews if she doesn't have AC? William said the whole thing was going to cost six thousand."

"That doesn't sound that unreasonable," Mama said.

"Maybe not, but after he's already gotten ten thousand out of us…I think it's unreasonable," Allen said with a dark look.

"Ohhh," Mama said, looking away. Turning back, she said, "And your sure you didn't go and talk to him?"

"No," Allen said. "Like I said, I planned to, but things are so crazy around here that I didn't get a chance to, and then on Saturday, Gary texted me and told me he talked to him."

"Mmmm, so that's what we saw," I whispered to Mama. She nodded her head.

"And Gary never mentioned going to see William's wife?" Mama asked.

"No," Allen said and stood up. "Listen, I really need to get back to work, okay?"

He started looking through the papers on the desk again.

"Well, we'll leave you alone," Mama said. "Thank you for all the information."

"Mm-hmm," Allen said, ignoring us.

We walked to the door, and Alexandra and I passed through it. Mama held on to the door and looked at Allen.

"Before we leave, quick question," Mama said. "What happened to that grey tow truck that Gary was driving yesterday? Did somebody come and pick it up from Faith's house?"

Allen looked up and frowned. "What tow truck?"

"Oh, we got something, girls. Come on back," Mama said, waving her hand at us.

Alexandra and I walked into the office, and Alexandra closed the door.

"Gary drove a tow truck to Faith's house yesterday," Mama said. "And it wasn't there when the police arrived. So, where did it go?"

"No tow trucks left the lot yesterday," Allen said, shaking his head.

"Yes, they did," Mama said. "Or at least one did."

"There was an eyewitness," I said. "Someone saw Gary and the tow truck at Faith's house."

"Impossible," Allen said. "Gary and I decided to give everybody the day off for Easter. Even though it would cost us money, we thought it was good for company morale. We were closed yesterday. No one took a truck off the lot."

"Hmmm," Mama said, looking at him.

"Okay," I said. "I guess we'll have to take your word for it. Um, one last thing. Where were you yesterday?"

"Really?" Allen asked, giving me a disgusted look.

"I had to ask," I said with a shrug.

He sighed and rubbed a hand down his face. "I was with my wife, at her parent's house, all day, enjoying my mother-in-law's cooking," he said in a firm voice.

"All day?" Mama asked.

"All day," he said with a bite in his voice. "Are we done here?"

"We're done," Mama said, holding up her hands. "Have a nice day."

Walking out of the office and down the steps, I turned to Mama and asked, "What do you think?"

"I don't know," Mama said with a sigh. "If someone was cheating my family, I would be mad enough to seek my own form of vengeance."

"Over that little bit of money?" Alexandra said in shock. "I know it's thousands, but it's not worth going to jail and losing your freedom."

"It is if it is all you got," Mama said, getting into the car.

*****

"Here we go," Jessica Hill said as she placed a tray with several glasses down on a table. "Some nice, cold lemonade."

"Thank you," I said, nodding my head as I took a glass from her.

"Mmm," Mama said, the ice clinking together as she sipped from the glass. She looked around the parlor. "This is a nice house. I had no idea there was a bed and breakfast in the area."

"Oh, yes," Jessica said, sitting across from us. "We've only been open a few months, but we are drawing quite a buzz. There is something about small town charm that attracts people, you know? And this town has so many sites that people love to see."

"Like what?" I asked in disbelief before I could catch myself. "I mean…I agree! Small town charm! Yay!"

I looked away and sipped my drink. (I needed to learn how to be quiet.)

"No, really," Jessica said, laughing. "There are the multiple fairs throughout the year, the multiple monuments, we have a lot of folklore that is important to the town, and we're close to other towns and cities. You can come here to relax, fish, and shop at small boutiques."

"Small boutiques?" I said. "Okay. Alright."

(I'm not in this conversation anymore. If we're not going to be truthful, then I don't want to participate.)

"You must be in charge of press and promotion for the bed and breakfast," Mama said with a smile. "So, you've been with Ashley since the beginning?"

"Yes," Jessica said. "She was looking for a manager, and I applied."

Another big smile spread across Jessica's face, and I just stared at her as I sipped from my glass. Jessica was a beautiful woman in her late twenties, tall with dark brown skin and a slim figure. She looked like the type who could have been a model but never got the chance to go beyond the invisible boundaries of this town. With a long bang wig that was pulled back in a low ponytail and dark-rimmed glass, Jessica was wearing a charcoal-colored sweater and tight-fitting jeans.

"Hmmm," Mama said. "Well, then I guess I should say I'm sorry."

"Excuse me?" Jessica asked with a slight shake of her head, her smile disappearing.

"No, I just mean I'm sorry about all the trouble you're going through," Mama said quickly with a wave of her hand. She sat back on the couch. "I heard the bed and breakfast was having a lot of trouble."

"Oh, well," Jessica said, looking away before turning back with that wide smile. (She really missed her calling for a toothpaste commercial.) "It's nothing. It's just those first-month pangs you feel when you open a business and you're getting your footing. It's nothing. Really."

"Mm-hmmm," Mama, Alexandra, and I said at the same time and then sipped our lemonades.

"We're—"

The front door opened, and we heard a woman call out, "Jessica?"

"Oh," Jessica said, looking at the door. She looked back at us. "That's Ashley. I told y'all she would be right back."

Jessica got up, and we watched her go to Ashley. Taking a store bag from her, Jessica leaned in, whispering.

"Now, if her husband didn't already call her and warn her that we were coming, then I'm booboo the damn fool," Mama said in a low voice.

"Mm-hmm," Alexandra and I hummed.

Ashley turned toward us and smiled. Shrugging out of her coat, she hung it up and walked into the parlor. At 5'7", Ashley had subtle curves and flawless caramel-colored skin. Her natural hair was in soft curls from a twist out, and she looked somewhere in her mid-thirties. She was one of those women who had a natural air of grace and class about her. Whether she was born a millionaire or was a small-town girl, Ashley was the type of woman who looked like she should be wearing pearls and sipping champagne.

"Welcome, ladies," she said, pulling down her cardigan as she walked toward us. "I'm so sorry I wasn't here to greet y'all. I had to run and get some more glasses. You know they don't make them like they used to. I trust that Jessica has treated y'all well?"

"Oh, yes," Mama said. "Everything is lovely."

"Good, good," Ashley said, sitting down and crossing her legs. She nervously picked at her nail. "Um, Jessica said you wanted to talk about my brother."

"Yes," Mama said, leaning forward to put her drink down on a coaster on the table. "We are private detectives, and we're investigating Gary's murder."

"I'm…confused," Ashley said, shaking her head. "I don't understand. The police are investigating what happened to Gary. No one in the family hired any detectives."

"No," Mama said. "The woman who is being accused of Gary's murder hired us."

"Oh," Ashley said softly. She looked at her nails and then at us. "I'm not sure how I can help you, and I'm sure you would understand if I say that I don't want to. I don't exactly feel generous towards the woman who murdered my brother."

"I understand, but we don't think she did it," Mama said.

"Then who?" Ashley asked, her eyes sparking with anger. "Who did it? Because she was the only one found with a knife in her hand, and she was the one found over his body."

"Who told you that?" Alexandra asked.

"An officer told my husband," Ashley said. She looked at Mama. "Answer me."

Mama held up a hand. "I know it looks bad—"

"Looks bad?" Ashley said in disbelief. She let out a little laugh. "Lady, you must be kidding me."

"Ashley, you and Faith are two women who are both hurting," Mama said. "She lost her husband yesterday, too."

"And she took her pain out on my brother by killing him," Ashley said. She shook her head and stood up. "Listen, I have a lot going on. I'm sorry, but I can't do this right now."

We blinked at her, feeling stunned at the abrupt way she threw us out. (It wasn't the first time someone had thrown out Mama and me, but it still stings each time.)

"Well, I'm sorry," Mama said, reaching to her right side and grabbing her purse. "I didn't mean to add to your burden."

"Mm-hmm," Ashley said, her face stiff.

Alexandra and I placed our glasses on the table, and we all stood up. We walked past Jessica and nodded our heads goodbye. She waved farewell and closed the door behind us.

"Well, that quickly turned sour," I said in a soft voice as we walked down the steps.

"She knew we were coming," Alexandra said. "Why act like that?"

"That was pain," Mama said. "It's too fresh."

"I wouldn't want to talk to us," I said, sighing. I looked at Mama. "It was a risky chance for us to come here."

"Yeah, but…" Mama looked at the house. Jessica and Ashley were standing at one of the windows and staring at us. Jessica had a comforting hand on Ashley's back while Ashley played with the necklace at her throat.

"Hmmmm," Mama said, a slight frown coming over her face.

"What?" I asked, looking between her and the house. "What is it?"

She looked at me. "Nothin'. Just hmmm."

"No, no," I said, wagging my finger at her. "You 'hmmmm' instead of 'hmmm.'"

Mama made a face. "What's the difference?"

"'Hmmm' means that's interesting. 'Hmmmm' means that my behind will be in some sort of trouble and in jail," I said.

"Oh, no," Alexandra said, waving her hands. "I draw the line at jail. I like you and your son, but not enough for jail."

"No one is going to jail," Mama said, rolling her eyes.

"Lies," I said.

"'Hmmmm' just means 'hmmmm,'" Mama said with a wave of her hand and walked away.

"Why do I feel a pit of despair in my stomach?" Alexandra leaned in to whisper.

"Because she's lying!" I growled.

Chapter Six

"So, any news about who bashed William in the head?" I asked, popping an elbow on the table to his right.

"A scorned lover? An angry client who felt cheated, perhaps?" Alexandra asked, appearing on his left.

"Maybe a very angry brother who was protecting his sister?" Mama asked from behind him.

Shay looked around and began chuckling as he poured sugar into his black coffee. We stood in Tommy's coffee shop surrounded by the soft sound of people's voices, the buzz of coffee being made, and the smell of fresh coffee filling the air.

"I knew it was just a matter of time before y'all found me," he said, tapping the stick against his cup and throwing it away. He put the lid on and smiled as he sipped his coffee. (Smug you-know-what.)

"Don't be cocky, Shay. It's not a good look," Mama said as he turned around to face her. "Do you have any leads on William's case?"

"I'm not talking about this case, Ms. Maven," Shay said, slipping past her and walking out of the shop.

"Now, hold on, Shay," Mama said, pushing the shop's door open before it could slam in her face. "Good detective work means not closing off any avenues. Why not work with us?"

"You don't want to work with me, Ms. Maven. You want to know what I know so you can go and try to solve this case," Shay said. He shook his head and pressed the button on his keys to unlock his car. "I'm not sharing any information with you."

"So, you're not even concerned about what we learned from Ashley Moore?" Mama asked.

Shay paused and then turned his head to us.

"I know you didn't…" He groaned and shook his head. "Ms. Maven, that woman just lost her brother. No, you didn't go and bother her."

"You talked to her," Mama said defensively.

"I'm the police!" Shay said. He put his coffee cup on his car's roof and fully turned to us. "Ms. Maven, leave this alone. This is a sensitive case for everyone."

"You know we're not going to leave it alone, Shay," I said.

"Not when our client is the one accused of murder!" Mama said, outdone. "We have to help her!"

Mama blew out a breath and looked at Shay. She held up a hand and said, "Okay, you don't want to tell me about your case. Fine. Can you just confirm something for us? We just need to know if Ashley was lying about her alibi? Can you do that?"

Shay leaned an elbow on his roof and rubbed his thumb over his bottom lip. A look of doubt and skepticism came over his face.

"Ms. Maven…" he said slowly.

"Ashley said that she was at her parent's house for most of the morning but that she went to her bed and breakfast at one to take care of some things," Mama said, knowing she had him. "Is that what she told you?"

"She said she left her parent's house?" Shay asked.

"Mm-hmm," Mama said. She looked at us. "Ain't that right, girls?"

"Mm-hmm," Alexandra and I said at the same time.

Shay sighed and shook his head. "That's not what she told me," he said.

"It's not?" Mama said. "What did she tell you?"

"Ms. Maven," Shay said, giving Mama a look. "I'm not doing this."

"Alright then, you don't have to," I said. "Let us guess. She said that she was with her parents and husband all day?"

"And that she never left?" Alexandra added.

"And did her people confirm this?" Mama asked.

Shay grabbed his cup and took a sip. He eyed us.

"Yeah," he said reluctantly. He cursed and then apologized. "Sorry. Now, I have to go back and question her and everyone else. I don't know why she's lying. Even with the stuff with William, she's not a suspect."

"Mm-hmmm," Mama said, nodding her head. She waved a thumb between the three of us. "We think it's the husband. He has an attitude. Big time."

"Naw," Shay said, shaking his head and taking another sip. He swallowed. "The former business partner that William cut out is more likely."

We blinked at him.

"Oh, yeah," Mama said slowly. "William's former business partner. Um…yeah…"

Shay looked at Mama and squinted.

"Oh, my God. Y'all lied to me. Wow," he said in disgust. "Really?"

"You act like this is the first time," Mama said, rolling her eyes. "You would think that you would be used to it by now."

"I mean…come on, Shay," I said, pointing a hand between Mama and me. "You know what this is."

"I've only known them for a short time, and I wouldn't trust what they say," Alexandra said.

Mama and I looked at her, both offended.

"I am so sorry," Alexandra said, her eyes going big as she looked at us. "That was supposed to stay in my head."

"Hmmm," Mama said, her lips pursed. She held up a finger. "That was your one and only."

"Understood," Alexandra said.

"Was anything you said about Ashley true?" Shay asked.

"God, no," Mama said, chuckling. "But thank you for telling us her alibi. Now about this business partner…"

"Oh, my God," Shay said, turning away from us. "I don't know what I did to deserve y'all."

"Okay, you're going to stop with all that," Mama said, holding up a hand. "You're acting like we're bad people, and we're not."

"We're just creative with a lie," I said.

"No, we don't lie," Mama said. "We like to reimagine the truth. There's a difference."

"There's literally no difference between those two things, Ms. Maven," Shay said. "Nada."

"Hmmm," Mama said. "Let's agree to disagree. Now, who is William's former business partner?"

Shay pinched his brow. "I'm not saying."

"Khalil Campbell?" Alexandra said. She was bent over awkwardly, looking through Shay's car's front window. "Or at least that's what I think it says. I'm reading it upside down."

Shay's mouth dropped, and his head whipped from his car to Alexandra.

"What the—? Wow! Just wow," Shay said. He pointed at Alexandra. "Two minutes in these people's company, and look what you've turned into."

"Hey, hey, now," I said. "You only get so many shots in a day. I'm gonna start hurting your feelings, too, in a minute."

"Khalil Campbell? Khalil Campbell?" Mama murmured. "Why does that name sound familiar? Wait. *Jan Campbell's boy?!*"

"Jan Campbell?" I said. "The woman who made me stuff all those eggs?"

"Yeah," Mama said, shifting her purse higher on her shoulder. "Well, technically, Khalil is her stepson. Jan's husband is fifteen years older than her and had a ten-year-old when they married, but she loves that boy like he's her own."

Mama's nose scrunched in thought. "I guess it makes sense. I know that Khalil learned how to do a lot of things around the house from his dad."

I looked at Shay. "So, why do you suspect Khalil?" I asked.

He sighed and gave up. "Khalil and William decided to partner with each other but started arguing about two weeks ago because Khalil felt William was cheating him out of money."

"How?" I asked.

"They worked on Ashley's bed and breakfast together," Shay said. "And unfortunately, a lot more work needed to be done on the house than Ashley originally thought, which meant a lot of money for the two of them, except William was taking sixty percent of the proceeds and only giving Khalil forty."

"Why cheat him if they were in a partnership?" Alexandra asked. "Was William desperate for money or something?"

Shay shrugged, a grimace on his face as he leaned against his car. "He was a working man with a family," he said. "But there's nothing in his financial records that showed he was in desperate need of money, and Faith said things were solid for the most part. Yeah, they had to be on a budget, but not that different from everybody else."

"So, William was cheating Khalil just because?" I asked in confusion.

"I'm not sure," Shay said.

"What does Khalil have to say for himself?" Mama asked.

"I haven't talked to him yet," Shay said. "I'm still tracking him down."

"He left town?" I asked.

"I don't think so," Shay said, lowering his cup. "But I haven't found him yet."

"Have you talked to Jan yet?" Mama asked.

"No," Shay said. "I talked to Khalil's girlfriend and a couple of his friends. I was on my way to Mrs. Campbell's house."

Mama's eyes started to glow, and a slow smile spread across her face.

"Mama, don't do this," I begged.

"Shay, why don't we go on….and, uh, take that ride with ya?" Mama said and started walking to our car.

"I don't need anybody to come along with me…." Shay's head turned away from Mama and looked at me. "What is happening here?"

"A mess," I said, throwing my hands up. "A damn mess."

*****

"Who is it?" Jan's soft voice floated from behind the door.

"It's Detective Shay Henry, Ma'am," Shay said, holding up his badge to the door's peephole.

"Oh!" Jan said. She opened the door. Jan was dressed in an old yellow housedress, an orange scarf wrapped around her hair, and her face was free of makeup.

"Detective…." Her voice trailed off when she saw us standing there. A look of confusion came over her face as she glanced at Shay.

"Afternoon, Jan," Mama said, smiling at her.

"Maven," Jan said, her lips tight. She straightened her shoulders and fixed her dress. "I'm not really sure what you're doing here, but hello."

"Oh, I'm just here to listen in," Mama said.

"No, she's not," Shay said. He cleared his throat and smiled. "Mrs. Campbell, as you are aware, I'm investigating the death of William Turner. I was hoping you would speak to me about your son, Khalil."

Jan's eyes widened, and she took a step back.

"You think Khalil has something to do with this?" she squeaked.

"No—" Shay began to say.

"Nobody said nothin' about that boy doing anything, Jan. Calm down," Mama said. "We're just here to ask you a couple of questions."

"Then why bring his name up?" Jan asked.

"Well, you see—" Shay said.

"Hell, Jan, what do you expect?" Mama asked, cutting him off. A look of frustration came over Shay's face, and his mouth tightened. "That boy William was murdered. Everybody he knows has to be talked to."

"I—" Shay opened his mouth.

"There's no reason to talk to my Khalil unless y'all are up to something," Jan said, pointing a finger between us. "I don't trust y'all."

"We're—" Shay began to say.

"Nobody thinks Khalil did anything, Jan," Mama said firmly. "All we want to do is talk to Khalil and see if he knows anything about what could have happened to William."

Shay turned and looked at me. He leaned in and whispered, "Am I invisible? Can you see me?"

"No, you're still here," I said, a small smile on my lips. "But you knew this would happen."

"It's just—" He jumped when Mama hit him on the shoulder.

"Don't just stand there lookin' pretty boy. Talk to the woman," Mama said, pointing a hand at Jan.

Shay stared at Mama and then rolled his shoulders to release tension from them. Turning to Jan, he smiled and said, "Ma'am, may I come in? If you have some time, I would like to talk to you about Khalil."

"He meant we," Mama said, drawing a circle in the air with her finger. "He wants *us* to come in and talk."

"No, I did not say that—" Shay said.

"For heaven's sake," Jan huffed, stepped back into the house, and held the door open. "Get in here. I don't need people wondering why the police are out here."

We walked inside, and Jan led us to a large screened-in patio. Colorful potted plants and flowers were everywhere, making the area feel almost tropical. A matching four-piece wicker patio set with overstuffed white cushions sat in the middle of the room. Alexandra and I sat on each side of Shay on the couch while Mama sat down in one of the chairs, placing her purse on her lap.

"Here we go," Jan said, coming back into the room carrying a large tray filled with glasses of iced tea. "Something nice and cool to sip on."

"Thank you," Shay said, taking a glass.

Murmuring thanks and nodding our heads, we each took a glass and sat back on the couch. Jan placed the tray to the side and sat in the other chair with her glass.

"Now," she said, touching her headwrap. "What do you want to know about Khalil?"

Shay put down his glass and pulled out a notebook. Flipping it open, he said, "When was the last time—?"

"Have you seen your son lately?" Mama asked, cutting him off.

Shay threw up a hand in frustration and sat back on the couch, his jaw working.

"I haven't seen him a week," Jan said.

Mama frowned. "He didn't come by for Easter?"

"No…" Jan admitted. "He was busy. I'll see him for my birthday."

"Busy doing what?" I asked.

Jan waved a hand. "Working," she said. "He's a very busy man. He owns his own company."

"What company?" Mama asked. "What does he do?"

"He installs floors," Jan said. She smiled at Shay. "He's absolutely fabulous at it. He learned it from my husband. Robert can do anything when it comes to woodwork."

"Mm-hmm," Mama said. She sipped her iced tea and eyed Jan. "Is that why he decided to start working with William?"

"What?" Jan said. She let out a little laugh and shook her head. "Who told you that?"

"Well—" Shay began.

"Jan, everybody in this town is talking about it," Mama said. "Supposedly, Khalil and William got into quite a row about money and the business."

"I don't know why I try," Shay whispered, shaking his head.

"That was nothing," Jan said, shaking her head.

"They weren't partners?" Mama asked.

"No," Jan said. "William simply hired Khalil to do some work on a bed and breakfast. Maybe there was some discussion that they could go into partnership with each other if this job went well. But the job didn't go well, and Khalil decided that he liked being his own boss."

"What happened?" Alexandra asked. "Why did it go wrong?"

Jan sighed and put her glass down. She leaned back in her chair and clasped her hands together.

"William promised to pay Khalil eight hundred dollars for the work at the bed and breakfast, but when it came time to pay, William only gave him five hundred," Jan said. She shrugged. "Khalil said William claimed it wasn't his fault and the owner cheated them, and that was all the money she gave for the job. Khalil didn't believe him, and they argued about it."

"Hmmm," Mama said.

Jan looked around, and her mouth tightened. "I know what you're thinking, but Khalil didn't kill William!"

"No one said anything about the boy killing William," Mama said.

"I can see it on your face, Maven!" Jan fussed. "Khalil didn't do anything. I was at church, and I would have seen my own son if he was there!"

"He could have slipped past you," I said.

"You—" Jan started and then snapped her mouth close. "You just sit there and sip your tea!"

(Now, we all know that I'm not drinking this nasty iced tea, but I will keep my mouth shut. There was no reason for me to get my feelings hurt when all I wanted to do was ask questions.)

"You must have seen something," Mama said to Jan. "You were outside getting things ready with Netta."

"I didn't see anything," Jan said. Her head tilted to the side, and her brows came down. "Well…"

"What?" we all said as one, leaning forward in our seats.

"I didn't see anything, so much as heard something," Jan said slowly. "I went to church early to put out the empty Easter baskets for the children. When I was walking back to the church, I overheard William and Faith talking, and he was cursing at her."

"Cursing at her?" I repeated. "Over what?"

"I'm not sure," Jan said. "He kept saying, 'How could you be so stupid?' and 'We don't have the money for this.'"

Shay frowned, and he wrote it down in his notebook.

"What else did he say?" Mama asked.

"That's all I heard," Jan said. "Church was starting, so I hurried to my seat."

"Hmmm," Mama said, leaning on the arm of the chair. "And when was the last time you heard from Khalil?"

"About a week ago," Jan said. "And he had nothing to do with this!"

"Okay, okay," Mama said, holding up a hand. "Calm down."

Mama looked at Shay. "You can go now," she said, pointing at Jan.

"Oh, me?" Shay said, pointing to himself. "Am I allowed to run my own investigation?"

"Sarcasm doesn't look good on you, Shay," Mama said. "Watch yourself."

Shay nodded his head. He turned and looked at Jan.

"Do you know where Khalil could be right now?" he asked.

"Have you checked with his friends?" Jan asked. "Or his girlfriend?"

"Yes," Shay said. He named several spots Khalil's friends and girlfriend told him Khalil could be. "But none of those spots panned out."

Jan sighed and looked at the ground. Raising her eyes to Shay, she said, "Try his biological mother's house."

"Who's his mother?" Shay asked.

"Rhonda Jenkins," Jan said. She shook her head and picked up her glass. "Sometimes, you can't stop a boy from loving his mother no matter how terrible she is."

Chapter Seven

"That's Khalil truck," Shay said, pointing at a black four-door truck parked in the front yard of an older house that had seen better days. It was a shame because you could tell that it was once a nice house, but years of neglect had led to peeling paint, overgrown grass, and old furniture in the yard.

"Are you going to go knock on the door?" I asked, looking at him.

Shay shook his head. "I can wait until he comes out," he said. He looked at his watch. "I have some time to kill."

"Mmm, okay," I said and leaned against my car. I looked at Mama and Alexandra, who were softly talking to each other.

I looked at Shay. "Do you think Khalil did it?" I asked.

"I don't know," he said, shrugging. "I need more evidence."

"What about Faith?" I asked.

"I don't know, Cookie," he said, looking at me. "She was over a body with a knife. You don't need more evidence than that."

I crossed my arms under my breast and crossed my ankles. We didn't say anything for a minute. Shay and I just stared at the house, listening to the sounds of children laughing, cars passing by, and the wind blowing through the trees.

"You know Mama and I truly believe she's innocent," I said, breaking the silence between us. I looked at him. "We wouldn't be doing this if we didn't believe that she was innocent."

"Yes, y'all would," he said, smiling down at me. His gaze returned to the house. "And you have every right to investigate, Cookie."

I smiled.

"Even if it annoys me," he said.

I lost my smile.

"Just don't be disappointed if Faith is guilty," he said. He shook his head. "Things don't always turn out as we want."

"Mmmm," I said. "Maybe."

The door to the house opened, and Shay straightened to his full height. Khalil squinted against the sun as he looked at us. Covering his eyes with a hand, he walked down the steps, and I got a better look at him. At the age of thirty, Khalil was a decent-looking guy with smooth skin and full lips. He was of average height with a medium stocky build, and his brown skin had a red undertone to it. A baseball cap covered his hair, but as he came closer, I could tell he needed a haircut from the bit that peeked out.

"Khalil Campbell?" Shay called out.

"Yeah?" Khalil said.

"I'm Detective Shay Henry. Do you mind if we talk for a minute?" Shay asked.

"About what?" Khalil asked, stopping in the yard.

"About William Turner," Shay said, walking closer to him.

"What about him?" Khalil asked. "He's dead."

"Mm-hmm, and did you have something to do with it?" Mama asked.

"My god, Ms. Maven!" Shay said, turning to her.

"Is this what this is all about?" Khalil asked. "You think I killed him?"

"No—" Shay said.

"Yes," Mama said. "Did you?"

"You know, I can go wait in the car," Shay said, pointing to his vehicle. "Tell me when you're done, and I can get out and come do my job."

"What's with the sassiness?" Mama asked, and she held up her hands. "We're partners!"

"No. We. Are. Not!" Shay said.

"Can we focus on Khalil?" I asked.

"No, we need to focus on your mother overstepping boundaries," Shay said. He pointed at Mama. "She doesn't know her place!"

Mama and I gasped at him.

"Oh, no, he didn't," Mama said slowly and with disgust dripping from her voice.

"Yes, I did," Shay said. "Ms. Maven, I have had it up to here—"

"How dare you talk to my Mama like that!"

"You big headed, wanna be—"

"I get you were the boss in your hair shop, but out here—"

"Y'all?" Alexandra said with worry in her voice.

"That's why your head is shaped like that!"

"There is a big difference between pressing hair and solving a case!"

"Y'all? Please?" Alexandra said.

"I dare you to say that to Mama again! Go on! Go right ahead and say it again! I. Dare. You! What are you gonna do? Huh?"

"Y'all! Please!" Alexandra yelled.

"*What?!*" we yelled at Alexandra. She jumped and clutched her purse.

"Khalil just got in his truck and left," she said, pointing.

"What?!" I said, turning to look at his disappearing truck.

"Great! Just Great!" Shay said, throwing up his hands in disgust.

Mama stomped her foot.

"Why'd you just stand there and let him get away?!" she fussed at Alexandra.

"Y'all were fighting!" Alexandra said, defending herself. "And I tried to stop y'all!"

"I am too through," Shay said, walking away.

"Good! Walk away! That's why your pants don't fit, discount boy!" I yelled.

Shay's shoulders stiffened, but he didn't turn around. He got in his car and drove away. (You know he was mad, he didn't even put on his seat belt.)

"Good one," Mama said, nodding her head in approval.

"Thanks," I said. "You know us Simmons stick together."

"Mm-hmm," Mama said. "But now we have a problem. Khalil is gone."

"We'll find him," I said. "And doesn't that show he's guilty? Why would he run?"

"He's hiding something," Mama said. She sighed in disappointment. "Come on. Let's go to the office and regroup."

*****

"Alexandra, as an honorary detective of the Simmons agency, I hereby give you the marker to write on the whiteboard," Mama said, presenting it to her before sitting down.

"Thank you!" Alexandra said, beaming.

(Yeah…Mama just didn't feel like standing up. Her feet probably hurt from those shoes, and she knows I've known her for too long to fall for something like that.)

"What do we know about the case so far?" Mama asked.

"Cases," I corrected.

"Cases," Mama agreed, nodding her head. "Good point. Should we start with William's or Gary's?"

"William's, I guess," I said, shrugging. I sat back in my chair and looked at the board over Mama's desk. "We found out Khalil was William's business partner."

"And that he was cheating Khalil out of money," Mama said. She waved a hand. "Jan tried to say Khalil was only considering going into business with William. I don't believe it. I think they were partners."

"Well, it doesn't matter either way. The point is that William was cheating Khalil out of money in both stories," I said.

"But don't forget that Jan said the bed and breakfast didn't have the money," Alexandra said, pausing as she wrote on the board.

"Mmm," I said. "Do you believe that?"

"William was charging them a lot of money for repairs," Alexandra said. "Maybe Ashley did run out of money."

"Good point," Mama said. "And there's Ashley and Allen."

I nodded my head. "Opening a new business can't be easy, and to feel like someone was cheating you? I know I would be mad."

"And I'm sorry to say it, but Allen does not come off as cute and cuddly," Mama said.

"But they have an alibi," Alexandra said. "They were with her parents all day on Easter."

"That doesn't matter," Mama said, shifting in her seat. "They all could have done it together."

"And then there's Gary," I said. "He could have killed William and then got himself killed."

"Hmmm, I don't think so," Mama said. She poked her tongue in her cheek. "I don't think he would have gone to Faith and William's house if he killed William."

"Not in a work truck," Alexandra said.

"Which brings us to Gary's case," I said. "We didn't learn anything new."

"Except that the tow company was closed, and Gary shouldn't have taken a tow truck," Mama said. "So, what happened to it?"

"And don't forget the other information about William's case," Alexandra said, tapping the board. "Jan said she overheard William yelling at Faith."

"Oh, yeah," Mama said. "But I don't think Faith killed William."

"Yeah, but what was the argument about?" I asked. I shook my head. "We need to talk to Faith."

"We need to talk to Khalil," Mama said, looking away from the board in disgust.

"At this point, we need to talk to anyone who knows something," Alexandra said, putting the marker down.

The door opened, and Ren walked in carrying several bags of food and a tray of drinks.

"Hey!" he said. "I hope you haven't eaten yet. I brought lunch!"

"Yes!" I said, getting up. "You are a godsend, Ren."

He stared at me.

"What?" I asked as I opened one of the bags and grabbed an onion ring.

"It's just…you don't compliment me often. It's scary," he said.

"Shut up," I said and bumped him with my shoulder while he laughed.

"Alexandra texted and told me the case ran into a bit of trouble," he said as he pulled food out of the paper bags. "What's going on?"

"One of our suspects ran away," Mama said, folding the paper down on a burger. She took a bite and said, "We're not sure what we should do next."

Ren looked at the board and said, "Khalil Campbell? Y'all are investigating him?"

We all paused and looked at him.

"You know him?" I asked.

"Kind of," he said, sitting down. "We were on the same basketball team when we were kids. How old were we? Maybe eight or nine?"

"Huh? He is around your age, huh?" Mama said, looking at the board, and she turned to him. "What do you know about him?"

"Not much," Ren said, chewing. "We weren't in the same circles in school, and I don't remember him talking much when we were kids. I do remember him being good at basketball as a kid, but that's about it."

Mama rolled her eyes. "Besides that," she said. "Were there any rumors about him? Anything you've heard over the years?"

"Mmmm," Ren said as he thought. He swallowed his food and said, "His mom is a drug addict."

"Jan?" Mama asked in shock.

"Naw," Ren said, shaking his head. He waved his hand to the left. "His biological mother."

"Rhonda Jenkins?" I asked in surprise.

"Yeah," Ren said. "I remember her coming to the school high as heck once. The look on Khalil's face…" Ren shook his head. "The coach had to convince her to leave. I think he gave her money or something. I remember him slipping something into her hand."

"Hmmm," Mama said. "And he's still attached to her?"

"You heard what Jan said. He loves her," I said.

"Interesting," Mama said, turning her head to look at the whiteboard. She turned back to us. "You know, we never talked to Rhonda. We just left her house once Khalil left."

"What are you thinking?" Alexandra asked. "You want to go back and talk to her?"

Mama nodded her head. "I think it might be a good idea," she said. "Maybe Rhonda knows what Khalil is up to, or better yet, where he went."

"It's worth a try," I said. I pointed at the board. "It's not like we have much right now."

"Mm-hmm," Mama said as she moved her burger to take a bite. "I hope so."

*****

"Can I offer y'all something to drink?" Rhonda asked, closing the door behind us. "I have coke and fresh lemonade? Water?"'

(Rhonda, I wouldn't accept a glass of water from this house if my Mama was on fire. Darnation, that makes me sound bad. It's not that the house was dirty. It's just…it had seen better days. Mmm, let me keep my mouth closed because y'all judge me, and I don't appreciate it. Oh, I can feel your condemnation when you're reading this. Don't think I don't.)

"No, thank you," I said, smiling.

"I'm fine," Mama said. "But thank you."

"The same," Alexandra said with a nod of her head.

Rhonda waved a hand to a large leather sectional. "Please have a seat," she said.

The three of us sat down next to each other while Rhonda sat across from us. Rhonda looked different from what I expected. Well, I shouldn't have had any expectations of her, but for some reason, I had formed an image of her in my mind, and she was far from it. She was a very petite woman. Standing only five feet tall, Rhonda was extremely skinny with deep lines etched into her dark brown face from hard living and desperate times. She had on a long curly synthetic wig with a blue headband that matched her long blue maxi dress and white cardigan. There was a gentleness about her that was calming. Maybe it was her eyes that looked so much like Khalil's.

"Thank you for letting us in," Mama said. "As I said, we only want to ask a few questions about Khalil."

"Anything to help Khalil, I'm happy to do," Rhonda said.

"Great," Mama said, smiling. "Have you talked to Khalil today?"

"Yes, he stopped by earlier," Rhonda answered. "He dropped some food off for me."

"Oh, that's nice," Mama said. "So, you two are very close?"

"Yes," Rhonda said. "I'm grateful for that."

"Why would you say that?" Mama asked.

Rhonda shifted on the couch uncomfortably. "I used to be on drugs," she said. "Really bad."

She looked down at the carpet and dug her toes into it. Looking at us, she said, "I basically missed his childhood. But…I had been on drugs since I was seventeen, and I didn't know how to stop. I *love* my son—"

"Oh, no one can doubt that," Mama said quickly in response to Rhonda's passion. "I can hear it in your voice."

Rhonda calmed down and took a deep breath. "Like I said, I love my son," she said. "I always have. From the moment I gave birth to him, I loved him. But I couldn't stop drugs, even for him."

She gave us a teary smile. "But somehow, he still talks to me, even after everything I put him through. He was there for me through all the times I tried to do rehab and all the times I failed. But this last time worked." Rhonda held up a finger. "*And* I've been clean for two years."

"Yes!" Mama said with a shake of her fist.

Alexandra and I laughed and clapped along with Mama in celebration of Rhonda making it.

"Thank you," she said, smiling. "It's the longest I've ever been clean."

"I'm happy for you," Mama said. Alexandra and I chimed in with our congratulations. "Khalil must be ecstatic."

Rhoda lost her smile.

"He's not?" Mama asked in confusion.

"No, no!" Rhonda said in a rush, shaking a hand. "It's not that. Khalil is very happy that I'm finally clean. But, um…I'm dying."

(Well, this was a tragic ending to the movie. I want my money back.)

"I am so sorry," Mama said, putting a hand to her chest.

"Me too," I said.

"Me too," Alexandra said. She opened her mouth but was lost for words.

"Thank you, but you don't have to say nothin'," Rhonda said, waving a hand. "I've lived a rough life. I'll be the first one to admit it. Hell, I'm surprised my body held up this long from everything I put it through. I've had my good times, and I enjoyed them. I just thank the Lord that I could get this far."

"Dang," I said. "Does Khalil know?"

Rhonda nodded her head. "I told him. He took it hard. Khalil tried to convince me to fight it, and I did, for about six months, but…there's nothing the doctors can do anymore."

"Do you mind me asking what it is?" Mama asked.

"My liver is failing," Rhonda said. She chuckled. "I didn't have any problems until I got off of drugs. Maybe they were preserving me like a mummy."

We laughed.

"Oh, that is morbid," I said.

"That's life," Rhonda said. She shrugged. "I've learned that you have to accept and laugh at the things you can't change. The other option is to get bogged down in depression and sadness, and I don't want to do that. I only have a little time left, and why waste it on something I can't change?"

"That's certainly a positive way to think about it," I said.

Rhonda nodded her head. "I just feel bad that Khalil is pushing himself so hard."

"What do you mean?" Mama asked.

"He's been working overtime, trying to make money to help me out," Rhonda said. "I'm going into hospice care, and Khalil is helping me pay for it."

"Oh," Mama said in a soft voice. "Then that drama between him and William Turner must have left a sour taste in his mouth, huh?"

"Are you talking about when he worked for that boy on the bed and breakfast?" Rhonda asked, a confused look on her face.

"Mm-hmm," Mama said, nodding her head. "We heard William was cheating Khalil."

"That's what Khalil told me," Rhonda said. "He said William told him some story about the owner not giving him enough money, and that was all he could pay Khalil."

"Mmm, it sounds like you don't believe the story," I said.

"Khalil and I didn't believe that nonsense," Rhonda said, getting up from the couch. "Y'all want some chicken? Khalil brought a full box."

"Naw, we good," Mama said.

"I personally think that the boy cheated him," Rhonda said as she moved around the kitchen. After a moment, she came back holding a paper napkin with a fried chicken thigh on it.

"Why do you think William cheated him?" Mama asked.

"The story just sounded funny to me," she said, sitting down on the couch. She started picking the crust off the chicken and eating it. "The owner would continually hire them and knew how much it would cost but then cheated them? But hey, maybe it was a good thing. That bed and breakfast was nothin' but trouble. Khalil liked it because it meant money, but Jesus, every other day he called me to tell me about something that was broken in that house. Something was wrong with the floors, with the toilets, with the oven, with the dishwasher, with the electricity, with the kitchen sink…whew! If I were the owner, I would have burned down the damn thing and got the insurance money."

We all laughed.

"Was it really that bad?" Mama asked.

Rhonda nodded her head as she chewed. "Khalil told me that he had never seen anything like it. That owner must have had the worst luck in the world."

"Hmmm," Mama said, looking away for a moment. She looked at Rhonda. "Did you and Khalil spend Easter together?"

"No, he—" Rhonda stopped and looked at Mama. "Now, wait a minute. What is this about? Why does it sound like y'all are asking if Khalil has an alibi?"

"Did I say anything about an alibi?" Mama asked, putting a hand to her chest, a hurt look on her face.

"I didn't hear anything," I said.

"Never came out your mouth," Alexandra said.

"All I asked was if you and your son spent Easter together? Is that wrong?" Mama asked, holding out her hands. "I'm sorry I was trying to get to know you better, be in fellowship. I didn't know there were sensitive topics I couldn't ask about. You should have warned me."

"Mmmm," Rhonda said, eyeing her. "Khalil stopped by here for a while on Easter."

"From the hours of when to when?" Mama asked.

"Oh, my God! You're like those annoying detectives on the tv shows!" Rhonda said.

"I'll take that as a compliment," Mama said. "Now, about the time he came over here—"

"Get out!" Rhonda said, waving her hands in the air. She stood up. "That's it! I'm not talking to y'all anymore! Out!"

"I'm tryin' to help you!" Mama said in disbelief.

"How?!" Rhonda said. "By blaming my son for murder?!"

"By trying to prove that he didn't murder anybody," I said. "Listen, Ms. Rhonda, we don't think Khalil killed anybody, but the body that was found at church is William Turner, and Khalil *is* a suspect. We're working to prove that he didn't do it, but we need to talk to him to see if he saw or heard of any issues with William."

"So, you're telling me you're on Khalil's side?" Rhonda asked, breathing hard.

"Absolutely," I said. I held up a hand. "I promise."

"Mmm," Rhonda said, not trusting us. She looked at Mama. "How about you?"

Mama held up her hand. "I promise too," she said. She sat back, crossed her legs, and rubbed a hand over her thigh. "In fact, I'm so much on your side that I'll give you a tip. If a big headed boy name Shay Henry stops by, don't talk to him."

I hit her with my elbow and looked at her. "Mama," I said in a low voice. "Stop it."

"Hmmm," she said, giving me the side-eye. She looked at Rhonda. "What I meant to say is…you should talk to him, too. It's just if you could delay it for a couple, or even several hours, that would be great."

"Mama!" I whispered through clenched teeth.

"You're not going to get much more from me. I remember what he said, and I'm petty," she said.

"Even with *murder*?" I whispered.

"No such thing as the bottom when I'm in a feud," Mama said. "We can go as low as you want to go."

"I don't know what you two are talking about, but it's getting on my nerves," Rhonda said.

"Let's get back to what's happening," Mama said. She pointed a hand at Rhonda. "We believe Khalil is innocent—"

(No, we don't, but we need Rhonda to talk to us.)

"And you have been a great mother to that boy—"

(She has not, and don't you judge me because she said it herself.)

"He feels closer to you than anybody else in this world—"

(Because he has emotional problems that need to be worked out in therapy.)

"I'm sure you know something that will help us," Mama finished.

Rhonda looked torn and then sat down on the couch. "He came by here around twelve," she said. "We spent a few hours together, watching tv and talking."

(Mmm, that didn't exonerate him from killing William. We had arrived at church at eight, and William's body was discovered around eleven-thirty, and it had been there for a minute. Khalil could have killed him, went home and showered, and then went to his mom's house.)

"What time did he leave?" I asked.

"Three," Rhonda said.

"Do you know where he is now?" Mama asked.

"Most likely with his girlfriend," Rhonda said. "They're expecting a baby."

(Uh-oh.)

*****

"So, I think Khalil did it," Mama said.

We sat in the car in front of Khalil's girlfriend's apartment, planning our next move. Mama had called around, and the church's gossip hotline had come through with the information we needed on where to find her. After driving to the apartment complex, we realized that we weren't sure how we should approach Khalil's girlfriend. She was pregnant, and we didn't want to stress her out, but she possibly had information about where Khalil was, and we needed to talk to her. Mama swirled her soda and ice around in her foam cup before taking a sip from the straw. I glanced at her before turning back to look at the apartment building.

"Not necessarily," I said. "He could be innocent."

"An angry man trying to help pay for his dying mother's hospice care, his pregnant girlfriend, *and* cheated out of money by a crooked business partner?" Mama said. "Yep, that sounds like the script of a good movie to me."

"I would go see it," Alexandra said from the back seat.

"Really, Alexandra?" I said, turning to look at her.

"Thank you, Alexandra," Mama said, looking at her in the rearview mirror.

"I'm sorry, Cookie, but this doesn't sound good," Alexandra said. "So far, the only suspects are him and Faith, and if you take Faith out of the equation, then…"

"You have him," Mama finished.

"He probably has an alibi," I said, waving my hand at the apartment building. "Y'all convicted the man and put him in jail."

Mama turned her head to me and gave me a look. (You know the one. The one that said I was simple minded and had gotten on her nerves. Yep, that one.)

"What alibi?" Mama asked. "I bet you a hundred dollars his girlfriend is going to say that he was with her all morning."

"That's an alibi," I said in a weak voice.

"From someone who is trying to save the father of her child," Mama said. She shook her head and looked away. "And please, Lord, don't let this be her first child."

"Oh, it's over," Alexandra said, shaking her head as she scooched to the middle of the backseat. She leaned forward and said, "She's going to lie on the stand for him."

"Mm-hmm," Mama said, shaking her head sadly. "There's something about that first child that affects a woman. You'll do anything for your man."

"Soul ties," Alexandra said. "At least that's what my momma told me."

Mama turned in her seat. "Speaking of soul ties, are you on birth—?"

"Mama!" I shouted. She jumped and looked at me. "The inappropriateness! My God!"

"I had a question, and I wanted to know the answer," Mama said.

"Alexandra, get out of the car! Grab purses and go!" I said, struggling with my door.

I stumbled out of the car and slammed the car door. Alexandra followed behind me, pushing my purse into my hands.

"Thanks," she whispered, looking back warily at the car.

"No problem," I said, adjusting my clothes and slipping my purse over my shoulder. "Sorry she did that."

"You will never have answers if you don't ask questions," Mama said, getting out of the car and closing the door. "All I'm saying is that I would like a couple of more years before becoming a grandma. That's all."

Alexandra and I groaned, and I cringed, feeling my cheeks heat from embarrassment.

"You're not going to stop, are you?" I said to her.

"I'll stop," Mama said, holding up a hand. "But my mind will keep thinking it, and more importantly, you know I'm thinking it."

She looked at Alexandra, causing her to take a step back.

"She's right," Alexandra whispered, looking at me in panic. "I can't erase it. It's stuck in my brain forever."

"Don't worry. If you plan on staying in this family, there will be a lot more embarrassing moments that will replace this one," I said, shaking my head. "You'll look back at this moment, and it will feel like nothing compared to everything else."

"Thank…you?" Alexandra said, tilting her head in confusion. "Was that a warning, or were you trying to comfort me?"

"I was giving you a glimpse into your future, Alexandra. *Look at it!*" I said, pointing at Mama.

"Put yo' damn hand down," Mama fussed. She rolled her eyes. "I would make a great mother-in-law. Wouldn't I, Alexandra?"

"I'm sure you will be a great mother-in-law…not that I would necessarily *be* your daughter-in-law…I mean, Ren and I aren't there yet…I mean, we've only been dating a few months, and you just never know," Alexandra said with an awkward laugh. She looked between Mama and me. "*Not* that I wouldn't love to progress to a deeper relationship with Ren. I'm just saying that you never know with relationships! It can be great and end badly. Marriage is such a big step! Am I right?"

Silence.

Alexandra cleared her throat and fixed her blouse. "So, we're looking for apartment 10A, right?" she said and started walking across the parking lot.

Mama and I followed a few feet behind her.

"I'm telling Ren," I whispered.

"You can tell him what you want to tell him," Mama said. "And what's he gonna do but nothin'? Huh?"

My mouth tightened. (Darn it, she had me there. If life was spades, Mama was always the big joker. She won every time. You can't beat her.)

"I think it's that apartment up there on the second floor," Alexandra said, pointing at a door.

We climbed the stairs to the second floor and knocked on the apartment door of Khalil's girlfriend, Tammy Edmonds. A few moments later, a soft voice spoke from behind the door.

"Yes?"

"Hi, my name is Maven Simmons from the Simmons Detective Agency. I am investigating a case, and I was wondering if we could speak with you for a few minutes?" Mama asked.

"An investigation? I don't know how I can help with that. I don't know anything about any investigations," Tammy said

"Are you Khalil Campbell's girlfriend?" Mama asked.

"Yes," Tammy said reluctantly.

"Well, our case has to do with Khalil," Mama said. "Do you mind speaking to us?"

"Um," Tammy said. "Okay."

I heard the lock click open, and Tammy opened the door slightly, revealing a young looking black woman. She had on a pair of large black framed glasses, a green strapless dress that showed her baby bump, and her hair was pulled back into a slick bun.

"May we come in?" Mama asked.

Tammy looked behind her and then at us. She opened the door and stepped back.

"Sure," she said, a brittle smile on her face. "Um, you'll have to excuse the mess. I wasn't expecting company."

"No problem," Mama said as we walked into the apartment. "You have a lovely apartment."

"Thank you," she said.

"These are my associates," Mama said and introduced us. She gave us a tight smile, and we nodded our heads in greeting.

"Please, have a seat. I'll just move this out of the way," she said, rushing to a loveseat and stuffing clean, neatly folded clothes into a laundry basket. She lifted it and walked to the bedroom.

We sat down, and I looked around. It was a nice place. The apartment looked like it had two bedrooms and two bathrooms. It was a standard looking apartment with those bland white walls that apartment complexes would never let you paint, or you would have to pay extra when you moved out because they needed to paint over the walls. The matching living room set was a light grey color, and Tammy had complimented it with a blue and white rug. There wasn't a lot of décor in the living room except for a few family photos on a bookcase against the wall.

Tammy came back into the room, smoothing her hands over her hair to smooth away the flyaways. Sitting on the smaller couch, she smiled and said, "Now, how can I help y'all?"

"Well, as I said, we're investigating a case, and Khalil's name popped up," Mama said. "We wanted to come by and talk to you."

"I'm sorry y'all came all the way over here," Tammy said, rubbing her hands up and down her thighs. "I don't know anything about any investigation, and Khalil is the sweetest guy. I don't know why his name would come up in an investigation. That's just silly. "

"Hmmm," Mama said, and she laughed. "I'm sure he is a very sweet man. So, you don't have any idea of anything Khalil could be connected to?"

"No," Tammy said, shaking her head.

"Hmmm," Mama said, a smile still on her lips. She leaned an elbow on the couch and rested her chin on her palm.

(Okay, yeah, Tammy's up to something. A. Shay had told us that he had talked to Tammy, so her pretending that an investigation was odd and coming out of left field didn't make sense. B. *Who opens their door to strangers and doesn't question them about the case?!* If someone came to me and questioned me about my boyfriend being involved in a case, I would at least ask the person what case they were talking about. Tammy has yet to ask us what we were investigating. She just started denying that Khalil was involved. Ohhh, Tammy. Girl, you messed around and told on yourself.)

"How far along are you?" Mama asked with a quick nod at Tammy's stomach.

Tammy looked down and rubbed a protective hand over her belly.

"Seven months," she said, looking at Mama.

"Ohhh, you're almost there, huh?" Mama said, her smile widening. "Excited?"

"Very," Tammy said.

"Your first?" Mama asked.

Tammy nodded her head. "For both of us," Tammy said, rubbing her belly. "It's Khalil's first, too."

"Do you know what you're having?" Mama asked.

"A girl," Tammy said, nodding her head.

"Ohh, a girl!" Mama said. "I have three of my own. Little girls are wonderful, and you get to dress them up like little dolls."

Tammy smiled and said, "I started buying clothes the day I found out what I was having."

Mama nodded her head and said, "I can imagine this is a scary time for you. A baby can cause a lot of stress. You start worrying about if you're ready. You start to think about your relationship and if it's solid enough to handle a baby. You start thinking about...making enough money to support that child?"

Tammy's mouth opened and closed several times. Finally, she shook her head and spoke.

"We're not worried about those things," Tammy said. "We wanted this baby for a long time, and we're ready for her."

"Mm-hmm," Mama said. "Tammy, where's Khalil?"

"I-I'm not sure," Tammy said. "He left for work this morning and should be back by five."

"Can you call him and see?" Mama asked. "It's really important that we speak to him."

"I try not to bother him during the day," Tammy said, shaking her head. "He's so busy at work, and I don't want to distract him from his job—"

We all paused when we heard a loud thump come from the small pantry next to the kitchen. Mama, Alexandra, and I turned our heads and stared at the door, waiting for something else to happen. Several heartbeats of awkward silence passed before Mama squinted her eyes at the pantry door.

Mama's head dropped back on the couch, and she said, "Please, tell me that boy isn't hiding in the pantry."

Tammy jumped up from the couch and said, "No, no…it's probably one of the can goods I bought falling to the floor. I knew I had overstacked them. I shouldn't have bought so many, but there was a good sale on them, and I—"

"Oh, this is just sad," I said, holding up a hand to stop her. "Please, no more. I can't take much more of this."

"After all the movies, television shows, and just life you two have seen, are you telling me that this boy is really gonna hide in the pantry?" Mama asked Tammy in disgust.

"No! I told you I bought too many pork n' beans…" Tammy said in desperation.

"This is painful," I said, looking at Mama. "I physically hurt for her right now."

"Like the police are going to come in here and magically say, 'Let's not check the pantry because the door is invisible!'" Mama fussed, rolling her eyes. She flicked her hand at the pantry door. "Cookie, go get him. I don't even feel like getting up for this nonsense."

"Will do," I said, getting up from the couch.

"No! please! Hey, you can't just open doors in people's houses!" Tammy shouted.

"Tammy, sit down and stop stressing that baby before you go into early labor," Mama said. Tammy looked at Mama in desperation. "Tammy, sit down. It's over."

I opened the door to find Khalil standing there, his eyes tightly closed and his body pressed against the shelves. (I don't know how he fit his big body in that tight, little space. That was a miracle in itself.)

"Well, this is just embarrassing," I said.

Chapter Eight

We all stared at Khalil. His eyes were still closed, and his chest was barely moving as he held his breath.

"Boy, get out of that pantry!" Mama snapped. "It's over! We can see you!"

Khalil opened his eyes and slowly let out a breath. He reluctantly walked out of the pantry, a few cans and bags of food falling off the shelves behind him. Tammy shook her head sadly, pain on her face. She mouthed the word sorry to him.

"It's not your fault," he said to her. Walking over to her, he put an arm around her waist and said, "I shouldn't have come back here. I should have left town."

"I don't know if you killed William or not, but I'm gonna need you to get better at hiding," Mama said.

"I didn't kill him!" Khalil said in a fierce tone.

"Okay, calm down. No reason to raise your voice," Mama said. She waved a hand at the loveseat. "Why don't you two sit down, and we can talk this out?"

"Why? So you can distract me while the police come here to arrest me?" Khalil asked in an angry voice, his nostrils flaring.

Mama and I looked at each other.

I covered my mouth and leaned over to whisper, "Someone is paranoid."

"The man squeezed himself in between a broom and Corn Flakes. Clearly, he's a little…you know." Mama whispered to me.

"Okay," I said, nodding my head.

"Mm-hmm," Mama said. She looked at Khalil. "Let's try this thing again. We got off on the wrong foot. I'm Maven."

"Beulah," I said, waving.

"Alexandra," Alexandra said halfheartedly. She turned to us. "Are y'all cases always like this? Because this is concerning."

"*This* is where you get concerned?" I asked her, my eyes going big. "After all you've seen, this gives you pause?"

"Everything else I could accept, but this…" Alexandra looked at Khalil and then back at us. "This seems like a lot."

"Mmm," I said, tilting my head in thought. "This isn't that bad. We've had worse."

"Hell, we've done worse," Mama said. "Remember the garbage can?"

"Or the cornfield?" I countered.

"Or that time you hid in the closet and that old lady beat your ass?" Mama started to chuckle.

I looked at her with a straight face.

"Oh, you mean the time you *abandoned* me, and I got my ass beat by a woman that was close to your age?" I asked, raising a brow.

Mama sobered. "You didn't have to say that," she said. "I am not that old."

"You're not that young either," I said.

"You know what, Cookie. You have one more time—"

"What's happening here?" Khalil asked, looking between us.

"Okay, you're right. We got off track. Have a seat," Mama said, looking at the couple. "And if it's any help, I don't think you killed William."

"You don't?" Khalil asked. He looked shocked as he sat down.

"No," Mama said, shaking her head. "I think you would have left a long time ago if you had killed him."

(Or he could just be stupid. Wait, I'm supposed to be on Khalil's side, right?)

"But that doesn't explain why you're hiding and running away," I said. "What's going on?"

Khalil sighed and nervously rubbed his hands up and down his legs. He looked at Tammy, and she shrugged.

"It's up to you," she said softly.

Khalil turned to Mama and said, "I…I was there that morning."

"Excuse me, what now?" Mama asked, slightly leaning forward.

"I was there. At the church," Khalil said. "I didn't kill William, but I found his body."

"Oh, good Lord," Mama said, leaning her elbow on the arm of the couch and covering her eyes.

"You *saw* his body?" I said. I turned to Alexandra and whispered, "Dial nine and one and be ready to hit that other one just in case."

"Got it," she whispered and slipped her phone out.

"Now, hold on," Khalil said, holding up a hand. He shook his head. "It's not like that."

"Mm-hmm," I said with a big fake smile. "Alex?"

"Ready to go," she said softly.

"What happened?" Mama asked. "Why were you at the church?"

"My mom invited us to go. She kept making a big deal of it because she was planning all these things for the kids and wanted us to be there to support her. At first, I told her no because Tammy has been having a rough time with the baby these last few weeks, and I didn't want her to be stuck at church for hours and be uncomfortable. But then, Tammy convinced me to go and surprise her," Khalil said. He shook his head. "I was running late, and I got to church after the service started. There was no parking, so I thought I would park across the street and walk to the building, but where I parked meant that I was walking towards the back of the church."

"From the church to the woods is a good distance," Mama said. "How'd you find Williams's body?"

"I was going towards the back of the church when I heard William shout from the trees. He yelled for someone to get off of him," he answered. "I stopped and tried to listen to see if he would yell anything else, but there was silence. I got a bad feeling in the pit of my stomach. I started jogging towards the trees, and when I broke through them, I saw his body lying there. I bent down to see if he was alive, but he looked…."

"I saw the body. He was very much dead," I said.

"Yeah," Khalil said. "Then I heard a noise from my right, and I took off. I thought whoever had killed him was coming back."

"Did you get a good look at the person?" Alexandra asked.

"No," Khalil said with a quick shake of his head. "I was moving too fast to see who it was. I wasn't trying to die."

"Why didn't you come forward?" Mama asked, bewilderment on her face. "Or come inside the church and tell somebody, or go to the police?"

"I panicked," Khalil said with a shamed look on his face. "I figured someone was going to find his body, and no one had seen me. So…." He shrugged.

"Mmmm," Mama said, shaking her head. "Mmm-mmm-mmm. What a mess."

She looked at him. "You and William also had problems, right?"

"Yes," Khalil said in a hesitant voice. "But nothing that would make me kill him."

"But he *was* cheating you out of money, right?" I asked.

"Yeah," Khalil said. "At first, I didn't want to believe it. William and I have known each other for a long time. But then, when it was time to pay me, he gave this bogus story about Ashley not paying him all of the money she promised for the job, and he could only give me a fraction of what he owed me. He didn't even try to say that he would make it up to me later. William just gave me a small payment and brushed me off."

"How did you know it was a bogus story?" Alexandra asked. "He could have been telling the truth."

Khalil shook his head. "A few days before William paid me, I was walking up the stairs, and I heard him and Ashley speaking in one of the bedrooms. I…there was a crack in the door, and I saw Ashley hand him a wad of money and tell him that this was the rest of the money she owed him for working on the house. She also said that she wouldn't be able to keep us on because we were too expensive and she couldn't afford it anymore. It was more than she had budgeted for repairs on the house."

"Hmmm," Mama said. "So, Ashley was paying William the full amount?"

"Yeah," Khalil said. "That's why I was so pissed at him. The first couple of times he came up short, he told me that Ashley didn't have it. But the last time I worked at the bed and breakfast, I saw Ashley pay him. It was a lot of money, and I thought he was going to give me all my money. Maybe even give me the back pay that I was owed." Khalil shook his head. "But he gave me that same b.s. story, and I couldn't take it."

"Did you two fight?" I asked. "Did you curse him out?"

"No, I just walked away," Khalil said. "I was too mad to deal with him, and I figured something bad would happen if I talked to him."

We looked at him.

"But I did not kill him," Khalil said adamantly.

"Hmmm," Mama said, eyeing him. She folded her hands and placed them on her lap. "Was the bed and breakfast really that bad? People keep talking about it."

Khalil shrugged. "It had good bones, but it had a lot of problems."

"Like?" I asked.

"Um," Khalil said as he thought. "The kitchen had several problems, and the bathroom plumbing needed to be replaced. At some point, Ashley would need to replace the wiring."

"Hmmmm," Mama said. "All that?"

"Hey, I wasn't mad at it having problems. It meant more work," Khalil said. He sighed. "Although, I regret ever agreeing to work on the place. None of this would have happened had I not worked with William."

Mama looked at him. "Hmmm. You need to go to the police." He opened his mouth to speak, but she cut him off. "You're only making yourself look more guilty by avoiding them. From everything you've told us, it sounds like you have nothing to worry about."

"Shay Henry is the detective on the case, and we've worked with him before. He'll listen to you," I said. "He's a good man."

Khalil looked unsure, and Tammy rubbed his hand.

"It's up to you, babe," she said. "Whatever you want to do, you know I'll stand by you."

Khalil swallowed hard and then looked at us.

"Are you sure he will listen to me?" he asked.

"Positive," I said.

"Okay," he said, more to himself than to us. Nodding his head, he blew out a breath and looked at us. "I'll go to him."

*****

"I'm arresting Khalil," Shay said.

Both Mama's and my mouth dropped.

"I can't say I didn't see that coming," Alexandra said.

Our heads snapped toward her, and she pressed her lips together.

I turned to Shay and said, "What happened? You were just supposed to talk to him!"

"I did," Shay said. "But some evidence came back that made it impossible for me to let him go."

"Oh, you're just being difficult," Mama said, waving a hand at him. "What evidence could you have against him?"

"His fingerprints are on the murder weapon," Shay said.

"Ohhh, that's not good," I said, turning my head away.

"Exactly," Shay said. "Add in the fact that he admits to being there, he had problems with the victim, and he has actively been on the run?" Shay shrugged. "I had to arrest him."

"You didn't have to do a damn thing but be black in this world!" Mama rubbed her face in frustration. "Okay, let me think. There has to be an explanation for his fingerprints being on the murder weapon."

"How did you even know it's his prints?" I asked.

"Khalil was arrested when he was seventeen for street racing with a couple of friends," Shay said, folding his arms over his chest. "His prints were in the system. When we ran the prints that were found on the murder weapon, his popped up and are the only ones on it."

"Darnation," I said. "Nobody follows the rules nowadays. See what happens when you don't drive safely! You get accused of murder!"

"I don't know how you made that correlation, but okay," Shay said. He looked at the three of us. "Listen, I'm sorry, but between Khalil and Faith, I'm closing my cases."

"No!" I said. "Don't do that! Khalil didn't do it! There must be something else! What about footprints? Or evidence that someone else did it? What about the eggs? Don't forget the eggs, Shay."

Shay shook his head. "The evidence points to Khalil. He admits to being there, and his prints were on the wrench. Plus, the easter eggs we found around William's body and his toolbox only had his prints on them."

"Toolbox?" Mama asked.

"Yeah, we found one on his toolbox when we were searching the bed of his truck. I think he must have taken some from the day before and then decided to slip out of church and go and hide them."

"Why take a wrench and not the whole toolbox?" Mama murmured, looking away.

"I don't know," Shay said, shrugging. "Maybe he was using it as a cover in case anyone came by? He could act like he had left service to go and fix something?"

"What about footprints?" I asked. "There must be footprints?"

"The crime scene was compromised thanks to everyone wanting to go see the body, so they could go back to their families and say they saw the body for themselves," Shay said, shaking his head. "You know how this town is. This story is going to be told for the next fifty years."

Shay shrugged. "Sorry, Cookie, but everything points to Khalil and Faith. I'm closing my cases. You two are going to have to face that you didn't solve this one and that I got the right people. I have to go," he said. "See you around."

"Oh, I curse you, Shay Henry," Mama yelled at his back. "May you always be stuck needing to fill your gas tank!"

Shay turned around. "That's just mean, Ms. Maven!"

"Good!" Mama yelled back. Shay threw up his arms and walked away, shaking his head at Mama's antics.

"Really? Gas?" I asked. "You couldn't come up with something better?"

Mama shrugged. "Have you seen gas prices lately? Filling your gas tank repeatedly is a curse no one needs right now. Come on. We need to go talk to Faith."

Alexandra and I hurried to catch up with Mama.

"Wait!" I said. "How are we going to talk to Faith? You know they are not going to let us in to see her."

Mama stopped abruptly, which almost caused Alexandra and me to bump into her back. She turned around and looked at me, a smile spreading across her lips.

"Cookie, where's your faith?" she asked.

*****

"Maven, I admire your desire to want to help people, and I'm even impressed that you decided to take on a new career after being a hairdresser. However, I'm not sure I like you playing with the Lord," Pastor Montgomery said, leaning back heavily in his leather chair and giving each one of us a disapproving stare.

After leaving the police station, Mama thought it would be a good idea to go see Pastor Montgomery for help. She said if anyone could get in to see Faith, it would be the pastor. It was a solid plan, except for one vital flaw. He didn't want to help us.

"Pastor Montgomery," Mama said, trying to put on a charming smile. "We're not asking you to break any laws or do anything morally wrong. We're just asking you to help one of your parishioners."

"And you have helped in the past," I added. "You saw how good that went."

"I wouldn't bring that up if I was you," he said.

I leaned back in my seat, feeling offended. (Oh, now he wants to change the narrative as if it went bad. See how people do you?)

"Faith is in a lot of trouble," Mama said. "We believe that William's murder is tied to Gary's murder, but we're missing a lot of pieces to the puzzle because we can't talk to Faith. If you could just…"

"The relationship between a person and their pastor is sacred," Pastor Montgomery said. "If Faith wants to see me, she should be able to speak to me freely as she seeks the strength of God in this tumultuous time without fear that whatever she discussed will be told to others."

"It's not like y'all's conversation would be private," I said. "The police are going to record you two and use it against her in court."

"Maybe so," Pastor Montgomery said. "But if I'm in the room with Faith, I will be giving her scriptures to read and counseling, telling her to lean on her faith and not on her own understanding of what's going on. I will not be a part of some gossip ring you three have going on."

He turned to the row of mahogany cabinets behind him and opened one that was full of files. Leaning over, he pulled one out.

"Good day, ladies," he said, dismissing us without even bothering to look at us.

"Oop, well," Mama said, putting a hand to her chest at the insult. "I guess I've been told."

"Mmm," I said and whispered, "See, if I put any money in the collection plate next time I come here."

We got up and quietly left his office, leaving the pastor alone to do his work. Walking into the sanctuary, we stopped to talk.

"Well, that didn't go like I planned," Mama said, disappointment on her face.

"It was a good plan," Alexandra said to Mama. "If he would have worked with us, we could have finally learned Faith's side of the story."

"What are we going to do now?" I asked. "Faith and Khalil are in jail, Shay is done with the cases, and I don't know who we should talk to next. We are running out of options."

"It's not over yet," Mama said. She put a hand to her mouth, a look of concentration on her face. "We just need to think of these cases from a different angle."

"What angle?" Alexandra asked.

"I'm not sure yet," Mama admitted. "Give me a minute."

"Mmm," I said, shaking my head and folding my arms. "What we need to do is speak to Faith."

"But how are we going to get in to talk to her?" Alexandra asked. "The pastor isn't going to help us."

"I'll help you," a voice behind us said.

Mama jumped and grabbed my arm, her hand going to her chest. She turned her head to look at Netta Dixon standing a few feet from us. Her large, curvaceous frame was dressed in a light brown satin top and dark brown slacks. With her hair brushed back into a bun and a slight touch of makeup on her face, Netta looked elegant.

"Whew, Lord!" Mama said, breathing hard. "Make some noise when you're sneaking up behind a person, will ya?!"

"That doesn't even make sense, Maven," Netta said, an annoyed look on her face. "How can you be sneaky and make noise?"

"Netta, I don't have time for this—"

"Wait! Ms. Dixon, did you say that you would…help us?" I asked, bewildered that Netta Dixon, *thee* Netta Dixon, would help us. (If you know the history between Mama and Netta Dixon, then you don't have to question why this sounded so weird to me.)

"Yes," Netta said. "I overheard y'all saying that you need to talk to Faith, and I can help."

"How?" Alexandra asked. She had the same confused look on her face that I was feeling.

"The church has a program in which we go to the jail and have bible study. I lead the women's group on Monday nights," Netta said. "You three can come with me, and I can try and make sure Faith is there, giving you an opportunity to talk to her."

"Oh," I said, blinking. I looked at Mama. "That's not a bad idea."

Mama's eyes narrowed as she looked at Netta. "What are you up to?"

I nudged Mama with my shoulder. "Mama!" I hissed. "This might be our best shot!"

Netta rolled her eyes, and her mouth tightened. "Why do I have to be up to anything? Why can't I want to help out of the goodness of my heart?"

A bark of laughter left Mama, and she slapped a hand over her mouth.

"Sorry," she said, the words muffled behind her fingers.

"You'll have to excuse my Mama, Ms. Dixon," I said.

"You don't have to apologize for me," Mama said. "I'm a grown woman."

I ignored her and continued, "It just surprised…us. You don't seem the type to want to help us on a case, especially considering…your past with my Mama."

"The past is the past," Netta said. "Plus, I want to help Faith. It can be difficult being a mother of four, and now she's a single mother of four. I don't believe she did it, and if I have to put aside my feelings for Maven to help that girl, then that's what I'll do."

"Am I not standing here?" Mama asked, looking around.

"Well," I said, looking at Alexandra and Mama, before turning back to Netta, "Thank you, Ms. Dixon. Your help is greatly appreciated. Mama?"

Mama sighed and sat down on a pew. "I can't believe that my life has turned to the point where I need help from Netta Dixon. These are truly the last days."

Netta smirked and walked forward to pat Mama on the shoulder. "I felt the same way when I had to turn to you for help. The pain stops after a while with a little Pepto Bismol." Turning away with a snap, she started walking towards the back of the church. "Now, y'all hurry up and help me bring these trays of cookies to my car."

Alexandra and I started walking forward, but I paused to turn back to Mama, who looked lost, and, frankly, a little disappointed with life.

"Are you okay?" I asked her.

Mama looked at me. "If I say no, would it make a difference?"

"I mean…I would feel really bad about it, but if you're asking me if I would still work with Ms. Dixon, then…" I closed my mouth and looked at her. (Somethings are better left unsaid. Why hurt people's feelings?)

"Exactly," Mama said. She let out a heavy sigh and got up from the pew. "Let's hurry up and get this over with."

Chapter Nine

"I really feel like this is illegal," I said, looking around the jail cells. "Has anyone looked into the legality of this?"

"I told you Pastor Montgomery worked it all out," Netta said, shaking out a tablecloth and smoothing it over a bench. "I don't know why you're stressin' about it."

"Woooow, you're really gonna put a tablecloth on a jailhouse bench? And then lay the cookies on it? Where people's asses have been? The toilet is right there. Not the soda! Okay," I said, turning away in disgust. "I'm sorry. I know this jail was built a long time ago and hasn't been updated to its full potential, but there is just something wrong with…all of this." I made a circle with my finger.

Women moved in and out of the cell, grabbing small paper plates and filling them with cookies. After each of them took a can of soda, they walked back to a larger cell that could accommodate all of them, laughing and talking to each other as they sat down and waited for the meeting to start.

"It's good for the women, Cookie," Netta said. "It allows them to have fellowship and look forward to something besides these dreary walls."

"Are they even allowed to be congregating like this?" I whispered. "They *are* criminals."

A woman stopped filling her plate and looked at me.

I let out an awkward laugh. "Oh, girl, I love your hair. Where did you get it done? Jail cell number four? Ha, ha, I'm just playin'."

She rolled her eyes and walked away.

I leaned my head out of the cell and pointed at her. "You walk that walk, girl! You are great! Great, I tell you! And the outside world is waiting for you!" I leaned back in and looked at Netta. "Get me out of here."

"Calm down," Netta said. "It's not like you haven't been here before."

I drew back and looked her up and down. "First of all, we don't talk about that. Second of all, I was on the other side of the cells. I know nothin' about this side. I've never been to this part of the jail."

"I'm surprised you and your mother haven't been here," Netta said.

"I think we're usually with people who have a quick turnover," Mama said, leaning against the bars. "You know, the ones they suspect will get bail soon."

"Hmm, not necessarily," Netta said, dusting off her hands. "This side is for those who are going to spend months in here or are still awaiting trial."

"Hmm," Mama said, looking around. "Interesting."

"What's Faith doing here?" I asked out loud, looking for her. "I would think she would be on the other side. Her case is still being investigated."

"From what I've heard, it's open and shut," Netta said. We looked at her. "I'm just saying what everybody else is saying," Netta said defensively. She grabbed a bible and walked out of the cell.

Mama walked out of the cell, and I followed her. Alexandra grabbed my arm and clung to it. I looked at her and frowned.

"What are you doing?" I whispered.

She looked at me, startled. "Nothin'," she said, trying to play it cool. "I just thought, you know, it would be a good idea to, um, walk in together. A united front in case there's trouble or something."

"Why would there be trouble-? Oh. My. God. You plan to push me in front of you and run for it, don't you?" I said.

Alexandra glanced at me from her peripheral and then stared straight ahead.

"You would do the same thing, too, Cookie," she said.

"That's not the point," I said. "I feel betrayed, Alexandra."

"You just admitted that you would do the same thing to me!" she whispered.

"Not the point!" I said, my nostrils flaring. I shook my head. "You never know someone until they are put to the test, huh?"

"Oh, no, you didn't," Alexandra whispered and looked at me with disbelief.

"Ladies!" Netta said in a loud voice, drawing everyone's attention to her. "We have some visitors with us today. I would like to introduce Maven, Beulah, and Alexandra."

The women waved at us, smiling, and a few of them welcomed us with greetings.

Netta leaned in and whispered, "There's Faith."

Mama frowned. "Where?" she asked as she tried to look around subtly.

Netta nodded her head toward the corner. "There."

We turned our heads to look. Curled up on the corner of a bench was Faith, dressed in her prison garb with her hair pulled back into two French braids. Her face was swollen from crying, and her eyes were closed as she leaned against the bars, her arms around her knees.

"It's only been a day. Jail got a hold of her like that?" I said. "At this rate, she'll never make it in the penitentiary."

"Hmmm, that is one girl that needs makeup at all times," Mama said, staring at her. She clapped her hands together and looked at Netta. "Alright, we'll talk to Faith, and you do your thang."

"Got it," Netta said, turning back to the group. "Ladies, please turn to Psalm…"

I tuned her out as we walked over to Faith. Mama nudged Faith's knee with her hand. Faith opened her eyes and rapidly blinked at us. She looked at us with confusion, opening her mouth to speak.

"You look like you could use some cookies and a drink," Mama said, cutting her off. "Come on."

Faith looked around, fear in her eyes that someone would stop her, and then slowly got up from the bench and followed us.

"What are you doing here?" Faith asked as we walked into the cell with the poopoo…I mean…Mmmm, Lord, help me. The *refreshments*. We walked into the cell with the *refreshments*. (Hell, y'all can't blame me. There's a toilet right there. I don't eat at people's houses if they have dogs or cats, and you expect me to eat next to a toilet?!)

"I told you we would take your case when you were in the back of that police car," Mama said. "What? You thought I was lying to you?"

"No, I—" She looked at the floor and shook her head. Tears started slipping down her cheeks. Faith looked at Mama. "It's been a rough couple of days."

"Oh, honey," Mama said softly and opened her arms. Faith walked into them and started sobbing, and Mama patted her on the back. "There, there, it's gonna be okay. I know it feels like the world is ending, but it's gonna be okay."

Faith sniffled and nodded her head. She stepped back, wiping her nose with her sleeve.

"Sit down and have some cookies," Mama said. "It won't solve your problems, but at least you can have something good to eat."

"Okay," Faith said, nodding her head as she wiped her face. She sat on the bench and grabbed a Macadamia nut cookie. Looking at us, she asked, "Do y'all want one?"

"Oh, God, no," I said before I could think. Mama hit me in the stomach with her elbow. "What I meant is that I wouldn't want to take these treats from you ladies."

"Faith, what happened at your house?" Mama asked. "What happened with Gary?"

"I don't know. After finding W—" Faith stopped and shook her head. "After church, I was in shock. My parents wanted to take me back to their house, but I wanted to be alone. I needed to gather my thoughts. My parents offered to take my kids and said they would drop me home. They didn't want me driving myself or the kids in the state I was in."

"Understandable," Mama said.

"When I got home, I laid on the couch, and then the doorbell rang. I got up and answered it. It was Gary, and he was yelling at me, asking me where the cars were," Faith said.

"Where were the cars?" I asked in confusion. I looked at Alexandra, who shook her head in confusion, too. "I don't get it."

Faith sighed and leaned against the wall. "He was there to tow away our cars. The last few months haven't been the best for us, and we're behind on bills."

My frown deepened. "I thought William had opened his own business and was making decent money?"

"He was, but it was too late," Faith said. "There was a long time when he didn't work before he decided to open his business, and I'm a stay-at-home mom. We tried to stretch things for as long as possible, but..." She shrugged. "We were behind thousands of dollars and having trouble catching up."

"That explains why he was cheating Khalil," Mama whispered, looking at Alexandra and me. "He needed the money for bills."

She looked at Faith. "The cars?"

"Gary came to the door, yelling about the cars. He accused me of hiding them so they couldn't be towed," Faith said. She looked at Mama and then looked away in shame. "To be honest, I wasn't above hiding them if I had known they were going to be towed, but I thought we had another month. I told Gary that I didn't know what he was talking about and that there must be a mistake. We didn't owe any money on the cars. I was trying to bluff him, but he said he had the paperwork to prove it. He turned around and left, and I went to my bathroom to get some aspirin for the headache I had. Between what happened at the church and him yelling at me..."

Faith closed her eyes as she remembered and then looked at us. "My head was pounding. It was bad enough that he was yelling at me for the same thing Will—"

She looked down, swallowed hard, and then started to nibble on her cookie.

"William yelled at you for the same thing?" Mama asked. Faith nodded her head. "Wait, did William say 'How stupid could you be?' and 'We don't have the money for this?'"

Faith nodded her head again. "We had a big argument at the church. He found out that I had been spending the car payments on the kids' afterschool activities."

Mama looked at her.

"I know," Faith said, holding up a hand. "I know. It's just…they were suffering, too, and it was hard for me to see them not be able to have the same chances as their friends. I thought it would only be a month or two at the most, and then I could juggle some money around and catch up, but W—he was out of work for longer than I thought, and I couldn't."

"It's a bit young minded, but I can't blame you," Mama said. "I can't say I haven't juggled a bill or two in my day. Hell, I don't know how many checks I tried to beat to the bank in the early days."

"You and William drove separately?" I asked.

"Mm-hmm," Faith said as she chewed.

"So, both your cars were still at the church," I said, thinking out loud.

"Yes," Faith said.

"How did Gary end up dead?" Mama asked.

"I don't know," Faith said. "When I came out of the bathroom, I went into the den, and there he was, laying on the floor. Dead. I ran to him and knelt to see if I could help, but he wasn't speaking. He wasn't even breathing. I stupidly pulled out the knife because I was in shock and thought maybe I could still help him. That's when y'all walked in and found me."

"Whew, Lord," Mama said. "Did you tell this to Shay?"

"Shay Henry? The detective?" Faith asked.

"Yeah, him," I said.

"I invoked my right not to speak," Faith said. "The police are just going to twist this on me."

"What about your lawyer?" Mama asked, concern on her face.

"She knows and said it would be my defense at trial," Faith said.

"Okay, I'm gonna be honest. I don't feel like your lawyer is the best," I said. "Do we know her?"

Faith named her lawyer.

"Who's her people?" Mama asked.

"I don't know," Faith said.

"Ugh, you young people," Mama said in disgust. "It's fine. I'll set you up with my guy, Bobby."

I looked at her. "Now you're calling Bobby 'your guy?'"

"Yes," Mama said. She smiled. "You don't know how long I've wanted to do that."

I shook my head at her, amused that she was excited about having "a guy." I turned to Faith and said, "You need to tell Shay all of this information. If he knows what happened, he's more likely to investigate the case than think you're the murderer and close the case."

"He's closing the case?!" Faith asked in a panic.

"Did I say that? I meant to say that knowing what happened will help as he investigates the case," I said.

"That was smooth," Mama said sarcastically.

"I'm trying my best here," I snapped. "I am standing in a jail cell, next to a dirty toilet, trying to solve a whodunit. Give me a break."

I looked at Faith, who was staring at me with wide eyes, and I gave her a strained smile.

"Everything's going to be okay, though," I said. "Remember, we're on your side."

"You sound like a cheesy salesman," Alexandra said.

I looked at her, losing my smile. "May you barber always cut your hairline crooked."

Alexandra gasped and stepped back.

"Stop it," Mama said. "Focus on the case."

"I'm trying, but I'm starting to smell things," I said. "Somebody get me out of this place. I think somebody is going to start braiding my hair again."

"Will you calm yourself?" Mama said, looking at me in irritation. She focused on Faith. "When you talked to Gary, did you see a truck outside?"

"A truck?" she asked.

"Yeah, like a tow truck," Mama said. "Did you see a tow truck at any point?"

"Mmm, I don't know," Faith said. "I was only focused on him and him yelling at me. Sorry."

"Hmmm," Mama said, putting her hands on her hips.

"What?" I asked.

"That little girl said she saw a truck," Mama said. "Faith said that Gary said he had the paperwork to prove that he had the right to repo their cars, and he turned around and left."

"He went back to the tow truck," I said. "You think someone was with him."

Mama nodded her head. "I think Gary was mad at William and wanted to get him back for his sister, so he jumped at the chance when the car company said to repo their cars. I don't think he would have gone there alone. You saw him and William arguing. They were evenly matched. You think William would have just stood there and let Gary take his cars?"

"No," Alexandra said, shaking her head. "Gary would have had backup. One person takes the cars, and the other one watches out for William."

"When y'all talked to that little girl, did it sound like a big tow truck?" Mama asked, looking between us.

"No," I said, shaking my head. "At least she didn't describe it that way."

"I feel like a kid would have described a big tow truck," Mama said. "Which means Gary would have had to take one car at a time."

"Oh, that is a fight," I said, nodding my head. "You're gonna take my car and then come back and take my *other* car? Ohhh, we fightin'. Mm-hmmm, I'm layin' hands, and they're not for blessings."

"So, who was in the car?" Alexandra asked. "When we talked to Allen, he denied anybody even took out a tow truck."

"Hmmm," Mama said, biting her lower lip.

"You think Allen is lying, or he doesn't know?" I asked.

"Well, it has to be somebody from the tow truck company," Mama said. "The truck disappeared by the time we got there. I think Gary went to the truck, the person stabbed him, and then drove away."

"With my knife?" Faith asked.

"What?" I asked as our heads all turned to her.

"It was my knife," Faith said slowly, shrinking back as if she was afraid to talk. "I recognized the handle. It's a plastic handle, but it looks like it's made out of white and grey marble. I got it for half off at Ross."

Mama groaned and turned away. Alexandra shook her head, held up a hand, and looked in the other direction.

"*Why does everything gotta be difficult?!*" I said in a loud voice, throwing up my hands in disgust.

*****

"Do you want to go and talk to Allen?"

"Mmmm," Mama said, not really responding. She sat on the couch with her eyes closed, her elbow on the arm, and was slowly rubbing her forehead, trying to ease the tension from it.

"Right, right," I said, nodding my head. "We should probably have a plan before we go and see him again. Do you want to go and talk to Shay?"

"Mmmm," she said, her forehead crinkling in pain.

"Do you want to call around and see if anybody at church saw anything?" I asked. "You know, tap into that gossip hotline?"

"Uh-uh," Mama said. She sighed. "All I want to do is eat, lay down, and not think about this case for a few hours."

"I get that," I said as I got up from a kitchen stool and walked over to one of the living room chairs. I sat down and leaned my chin on my fist. I blew out a breath, looked around the living room, sighed a couple of times, and then started to hum.

"If you don't stop that," Mama said. Her head rose, and she looked at me. "If you got nervous energy, I can give you something to do. My kitchen needs to be cleaned. You can go do that."

I straightened up in my seat, feeling offended. "Fine. I will stop."

"Thank. You," Mama said, rolling her eyes and going back to rubbing her forehead.

A few seconds passed before I felt myself burst. "It's just that I think Allen is the murderer, and we should go to the tow truck company and prove it!" I said to her.

Mama gave me a look. "Why can't you be quiet like that one in the corner?" she asked, pointing to Alexandra on the other end of the couch.

Alexandra gave us a weak smile. "I've been trying to plan my exit for the last twenty minutes, but nothing is working, so I'm just going to leave. Thank you so much for including me in your investigation. Don't call me again."

She started to get up from the couch, but Mama stopped her with a wave of her hand.

"No, Cookie is right," she said. "We need to figure this out. Clearly, Allen is involved in some way."

"Exactly! William was cheating his wife. Both he and Gary were pissed about it. They probably went to William and Faith's house to get revenge on them or be petty, and something went wrong!" I said, counting off the reasons on my fingers. "He's our best suspect! He probably killed William, too, and Ashley and his in-laws are covering for him. Ha!"

Mama shifted on the couch and blew out a breath. "It's not a bad theory," she said.

"It's after seven," I said. "The tow truck place is closed. We should go and look around."

"No, we'll go first thing in the morning," Mama said. "I don't feel like sneaking around tonight. I have a headache."

She looked at Alexandra. "How many sick days do you have at work?"

"What?" Alexandra asked, blinking at Mama.

"How many sick days do you have at work?" Mama repeated. "You should go with us tomorrow. See the case through."

"What? Nooo," Alexandra said, dragging the word out. She laughed. "I-I-It's been fun. But I don't want to intrude." She pointed a hand at me. "This is a you and Cookie thing. Not a you, Cookie, and Alexandra thing. It wouldn't be right."

"Naw," Mama said. "I like the idea of you on the case. As a woman, you should always see something through to the end. It builds character."

"I—" Alexandra closed her mouth and chuckled again. She looked at me for help. I smiled and leaned on the arm of my chair, enjoying the show.

"Yeah, Alexandra. It builds character," I said.

"You know, I would call out, but there is a big presentation at work tomorrow, and then I also, um, I also promised Ren that we would spend time together. Yeah. We, um, haven't seen each other as much as we would have liked to because of this big presentation, and I promised him that when I was done, we would spend the evening together…on a romantic date. Yeah," Alexandra said, nodding her head.

"God, I love this," I said, smiling as I rested my cheek in the palm of my hand.

"I can understand that. What time is your presentation?" Mama asked.

"Mmm?" Alexandra asked.

"She asked, 'what time is your presentation?'" I said. "Mmm-hmm, that's what she asked."

Alexandra looked at me and shook her head. (Oh, I got that look many times from my siblings.)

Alexandra turned to Mama. "Um, it's at…nine. Yep, nine a.m.," she said.

"Perfect," Mama said, holding out her hands, a smile spreading across her face. "You can give your presentation, and we'll pick you up right after. Just say you have a migraine and need to go home."

"I…ohhh, um…I don't really like to lie to my boss about those things…what if I get a real migraine in the future?" Alexandra said. "You know my momma always told me about the boy who cried wolf. Ha, ha, ha."

"But Alexandra, Marques told me that Ren told him that you lied to your boss so you and he could go on a romantic boat ride where you, quote, wore a new sexy black bikini just for him, end quote," I said.

Mama looked at her. "So, I guess that means you will be here at nine?"

Alexandra's eyes narrowed at me. I smiled.

"Next time, you won't try to push me in front of you in a prison riot, huh?" I said.

"We weren't in a prison riot!" Alexandra snapped.

"Not the point," I said.

Alexandra looked at Mama. She pushed a pillow off her lap and gathered her courage.

"Ms. Maven, I don't want to work on the case anymore," she said. "It has been very nice, and thank you for the opportunity, but I really think this career is better suited for you and Cookie."

"No," Mama said simply.

Both Alexandra and I looked at her in shock.

"No?" Alexandra asked in disbelief.

"Now, wait a minute," I said, holding up a hand. "I was just messing with Alexandra. How can you tell her no? You can't force her to be here if she doesn't want to."

"It's not about her," Mama said. "It's about Ren. I refuse to let that boy dictate my business. He called me early this morning about not letting Alexandra get into anything 'foolish.'"

"Ohhh, he did not use the word foolish," I said, my head dropping. (I loved my brother, but he could be stupid sometimes.)

"What does he mean, 'let me?'" Alexandra asked, offended. "But he brought us lunch? And was texting me all day?"

"No, he brought you lunch," Mama said, pointing a finger at her. "Cookie and I were just lucky bystanders. He was checking up on you."

"Ohhh," Alexandra said, her body vibrating.

"Alexandra, calm down," I said. "It's actually sweet if you think about it."

"I am a grown woman who is capable of taking care of herself!" Alexandra declared. "He could have communicated with me his concerns instead of making me think that he was just being all…"

"An overbearing jackass?" I asked.

Alexandra stopped and looked at me. "I was going to say my sweet and cuddly lovebug."

"Lovebug?" Mama and I said at the same time.

Mama turned her head to hide her laughter.

"Good Lord," I said in disgust. "Please reframe from telling me any more pet names you two have for each other."

"Ms.Maven," Alexandra said, sitting up proudly. "You can expect me here at nine sharp. Do y'all want coffee or orange juice with y'all's breakfasts?"

Mama smiled.

Chapter Ten

The next morning, we stood in front of the tow truck company. People were moving around the lot, climbing in and out of trucks, and the harsh sound of the gate opening to allow a truck to pass through came from our left.

"What's the game plan?" I asked, turning my head to look at Mama and Alexandra.

"We're going to go in, play it cool, and see if we can crack Allen," Mama said. "Hopefully, we can find some evidence to bring to Shay to prove that he killed Gary."

"And maybe even William," I said.

Mama nodded her head, and we started walking forward.

"Excuse me," Mama said, stopping a tall, Mexican-American man with a shaved head and a clean-shaven face. She gave him a charming smile. "Is Allen around?"

"We have two Allens who work here. Which one are you looking for?" he asked.

"Allen Moore," Mama said.

"He's out on a tow," the guy said. "Can I help you with something?"

"Um," Mama said, looking around. "Naw, it's okay. We'll wait until he gets back."

"Wait," the guy said, pointing at us with his pen. "Are you the three who are the investigators?"

Mama's eyebrows rose. "You've heard of us?"

"People couldn't stop talking about you three when I got back here yesterday," he said, chuckling. "Y'all caused a stir. It seems like y'all got on Allen's nerves. He fussed for a good hour after ya'll left, and it's hard to get under Allen's skin."

"Are you sure? That man seems like he got bad nerves," I said.

He laughed. "I'm sure. Allen doesn't let a lot of things get to him."

"What's your name?" Mama asked.

"Max," he said, holding out his hand for each of us to shake.

"Nice to meet you, Max," Mama said. She introduced the three of us, and he nodded his head at us. "Have you worked here a long time?"

"About three years," he said.

"Good place to work?" Mama asked, a sly look in her eyes. "Is Allen a good boss? What about Gary?"

"Nice try, but I'm not talking," he said.

"You don't even know what we're investigating," I said. "How do you know you don't want to talk to us?"

"Listen, Allen's a good guy. I don't know why you're harassing him," Max said.

"What? It's suddenly illegal to come by twice?" Mama asked.

"You and the cops?" Max asked. He shook his head. "Come on."

I tilted my head. "The cops were back here?"

"Yeah, this morning. From what I heard, that same detective from yesterday," Max said.

"Shay," Mama and I said at the same time, our eyes narrowing. We looked at each other, silently communicating.

Mama looked at Max. "I'm sorry you feel like we're harassing Allen because we're not. We're trying to help. We want to figure out who killed his brother-in-law, Gary."

"Yeah," Max said, looking at the ground. He blew out a breath and crossed his arms. "It's a shame. Gary was a good guy. He took care of his family and was a fair boss."

"Lovely," Mama said. "Is it company policy to take tow trucks out by yourself on y'all's days off?"

Max's brows came down in confusion. "What are you talking about?"

"You know, if y'all got a call when the company was closed, would one of you take it?" Mama asked.

Max gave her a strange look. "The company is closed. No one works on their off day."

"So, it would be really odd for a tow truck to be out when the company was closed?" Mama asked.

"Yes," Max said, slowly as if he was talking to someone who wasn't the brightest bulb.

"Do y'all keep records of the tow trucks' movements? Like a tracking device or something?" Mama asked.

"No," Max said. "We keep records of the calls we are sent out on, but there aren't any tracking devices on the trucks—"

"Hey, Max! I finished cleaning those trucks! See you next week!" a man yelled, interrupting our conversation.

"Alright, Shad! Thanks, man! See you next week!" Max yelled back, raising his hand in the air in goodbye.

We turned around to see a man hanging out of a white van. The words, Brenner's Mobile Car Wash, was painted on its side. Shad straightened in the van and pushed the gas, disappearing through the gates and leaving us in a world of confusion.

"What the what?" I said, my head going back and forth. I swirled back to Max and pointed where the van used to be. "That said Brenner's Mobile Car Wash."

"Yeah?" Max said, not seeing my point.

"Gary had his mobile car wash company cleaning the tow trucks?" Mama asked.

"Yeah," he said. Max shrugged. "It was a smart move. It kept money in his car wash company, and the tow trucks got a discount on car washes."

"Was that normal?" Alexandra asked. "What I mean is, is today the regular day that they're supposed to be cleaning trucks?"

"Mmm, not really," Max said, crossing his arms. A look of concentration appeared on his face."I think Allen called them in because a spill happened in one of the trucks. He tried yesterday, but they were closed because of…well, you know, Gary's death."

"He called them yesterday to come and clean one of the trucks?" Mama said, her voice going up an octave. "Oop!"

Mama, Alexandra, and I took off running in the direction that the van had come from and then stopped in our tracks before running back to Max.

"Where are the trucks he cleaned?" I asked.

"They're in the back, but it's restricted to employees," Max said. "What is y'all's problem?"

"Take us," Mama said, waving an encouraging hand. "Come on"

"I'm not taking you—"

"*Boy, this is a matter of life or death! Your sick-minded boss could have plotted the murder of your other boss with a marble-handled knife from Ross that was gotten on discount and then used the victim's own company to clean up the crime scene!*" Mama shouted.

The whole area went quiet as people turned to look at us. Max had a look on his face of both fear and indecision on whether he should call the police on us. Mama shifted her shoulders and straightened her green blazer.

"I apologize for yelling at you," Mama said, trying to be dignified in the awkward situation. "But I believe it is pertinent to the situation that you show us where the truck is because we believe it is a valuable piece of evidence in our investigation."

I leaned over and whispered, "Nice save, Mama. You're cool like a cucumber."

Her eyes cut to me. "Not now, Cookie," she said in an annoyed voice.

"I'll take you there, okay?" Max said. (I think he was more concerned that we were some lunatics and thought it was easier to give us our way.) "Just calm down, alright?"

"Yes," Mama said, nodding her head. "And don't act like I'm the only one to act like this around here. I'm sure plenty of you have shown your natural-born behinds around here."

Max held up his hands. "I didn't say anything," he said.

"Mmm, well, you just go ahead and take us," Mama said, still embarrassed.

"Alright," he said.

He started walking, and we followed him to the back of the building. A small lot was surrounded by brown and green grass, slowly dying from a lack of water. Three tow trucks were lined up in the lot, each with the company's name and logo on the side, and water droplets hung from the trucks, sparkling underneath the bright sun.

"This is it," Max said, waving a hand at them before putting his hands in his pockets. "I don't know what you expected to see."

"Can we look at them?" I asked. "I mean, can we look inside?"

Max looked at the trucks, indecision on his face. Finally, he nodded his head. "Sure. Just don't touch anything. The last thing I need is for something to break on them."

We rushed to the trucks. Opening the doors, we climbed inside and desperately started looking for clues. When we were in the last truck, and nothing had been found, I slammed my hand on the seat in frustration.

"Nothing," I said. I looked at Mama, and she shook her head. "You think the cleaners did that good of a job?"

"No," Mama said, shaking her head. She sat in the seat and looked around. "There has to be something here. There has to be! It's too much of a coincidence that Allen would want to clean these trucks a day *after* Gary was killed."

"Mmm," I said, my face scrunched as I thought.

"Hey! What's going on here?!" a loud, angry voice said behind us.

"Ohh," I said, jumping at the voice, my foot almost slipping from the truck. I grabbed the seat and pulled myself up. Turning around, I saw Allen looking at us, a mixture of anger and irritation on his face

"What are y'all doing in my truck?" he shouted.

"First of all, I'm less than five feet from you. You don't have to yell," I said. "And second, *what are you hiding, sir?!*"

He jumped at the volume of my voice."You just yelled at me!" he said in disbelief.

"Because you are out here cleaning trucks days after your brother-in-law was murdered?! Suspicious!" I said.

He gave me a look that said he thought I was an idiot and then looked at Mama. "Okay, is there an adult here that I can talk to?" he asked her.

My mouth dropped open, and I looked at her. "I'm insulted, but I did come in kinda hot, huh?"

She patted me on the thigh. "You did, but I wasn't mad at it," she said. She looked at Allen. "Cookie made a very good point. Why did you have these trucks cleaned?"

"Why did I—? I don't have to justify why I wanted to get my trucks cleaned?! Are you crazy?" Allen shouted.

"He's yelling again," I said. "I'm literally right next to him. I can reach out and touch him with my foot."

"Out!" Allen said, getting fed up with us. He pointed at the gate.

"We don't have to leave if we don't want to—" Mama started.

"*Now!*" Allen yelled.

"Ohh! Ohh, Lord, he put the deep baritone in that one. Okay, let's go," Mama said, climbing out of the truck. "We're going. We're going!"

Allen gave us an angry look as we passed, and he slammed the truck door close. We got to our car and then looked back at the company. It felt like an invisible barrier had risen between us and any access we would have to question Allen.

"Now what?" Alexandra said. "He's not going to let us back in there."

"No," Mama said slowly. "But there's somebody he can't say no to."

*****

"You know calling me only when you need me is starting to get old," Shay said as he closed his car door.

"We don't only call you when we want something," Mama said. "We have called you plenty of times just to talk and see how you're doing."

"When?" Shay challenged.

"Well, there was that time—" Mama stopped and looked at me. I slightly shook my head, and she turned back to him. "No, remember when—? Now, don't lie. Last month, I called to see—? Hmmm. Well, why the heck would I call a child to talk? I talk to grown folks! You need to focus on this boy and his tow truck cleaning antics and worry less about telephone games."

"That's right, Mama, if you're not in the right, hit them with anger," I said, punching an imaginary victim.

Mama rolled her eyes while Shay smiled as he took off his sunglasses and hooked them on his shirt.

"What's going on?" he asked.

"Okay, listen," I said. "Allen told us that he knew nothing about Gary taking a tow truck to Faith's house, but when we came today, he had three of his trucks cleaned which is very suspicious because it's not the normal day he gets them cleaned. Plus, one of his workers told us that he wanted to get the truck cleaned the day after Gary was killed by Gary's mobile carwash company but couldn't because they were closed. He claims there was a spill in one of the trucks, and that's why he wanted to get it cleaned."

"That's not a lot," Shay said with a shrug. "It's odd, but not enough for me to go in there and talk to him again after talking to him this morning."

"But Faith said Gary was fine when he showed up at her house and wanted to tow her cars. When she came back from the bathroom, he was stabbed and dying on her floor. We think someone was with Gary to make the tow. What if the person who was with Gary was the one who killed him?" I asked.

Shay didn't say anything for a minute or two. Then his head lifted, and he asked, "When did you talk to Faith?"

"Huh?" I said, blinking.

"You said, 'Faith said.' When did you talk to Faith?" he asked again.

"Oh, my God," I said, turning away.

"You're concentrating on that at a time like this?!" Mama asked in disbelief.

"I gave special instructions for you two not to be allowed in the cells. Who let y'all go down there?" Shay asked, not giving up.

"The Lord," Mama said with a straight face.

Shay gave her an annoyed look. "The Lord?" he asked.

"Hey," Mama said, holding up her hands. "Take it up with Him. He has the final say."

"Mmm, alright," Shay said. He doubled-tapped the top of our car and turned around to walk to the gate.

"Where are you going?" I yelled.

"To talk to Allen. Alone!" he said.

"Oop," Mama said, shutting her mouth. We watched him walk across the lot and up to the office. He knocked on the door and then disappeared inside.

"I wonder if he's going to tell us what he learned," Alexandra said. "I hope he does."

Mama smacked her lips. "Girl, please. Come on."

"It's about time. I was wondering what was taking you so long," I said as we walked across the lot.

We walked up the stairs, and Mama opened the door.

"There is nothing wrong with me cleaning my trucks—" Allen stopped and looked at us. "Oh, you have got to be kidding me."

Shay glanced at us and looked up at the ceiling, his jaw tightening.

"Excuse me. Thank you," Mama said, pushing Shay over. He moved a bit so we could all fit into the tight office.

"I thought I told y'all to get off my property?" Allen said.

"We're here on official police business," Mama said, looking smug. She hit Shay on the arm. "Ain't that right?"

"It's not right. They are not here with me," he said to Allen.

"In fact, he invited us," Mama said.

"I would never say those words," Shay said.

"He knows how good we are when it comes to investigating cases," Mama said.

"Mmmm?" Shay said, scrunching his face. "I would say, yes, you two investigate. Good at it?"

"He is a respected detective and has high respect for us, too," Mama said.

"I want to get into heaven, so I'm not going to disrespect my elders," Shay said.

"Exactly," Mama said, nodding her head. (What conversation did she hear? Because the one I heard wasn't flattering at all.)

"What is it that y'all want?" Allen asked.

"Answer the question. Why did you get the trucks cleaned?" I asked.

"Because I can," Allen said with an attitude. "But if you must know, one of them had a bad spill in it, and I figured I would get the other two cleaned while the cleaners were here."

"Hmm, a spill, huh? Would that spill be blood?" Mama asked.

"No, it was cranberry juice," Allen said.

"Cranberry juice? That sounds convenient," I said.

"No, it sounds like Gary didn't know how to close a bottle properly," Allen said.

"Gary? So, he did take out a tow truck on Sunday," Mama said.

"No, I told you that we were closed on Sunday," Allen said. "But he did do tows on Saturday. When I got here on Monday, one of the workers told me that the passenger seat was full of cranberry juice. I guess Gary left a bottle of it on the seat and didn't tighten it properly. It spilled all over the damn place."

"How do you know it was Gary?" I asked.

"I'm assuming it was Gary," Allen said with a shrug. "He was the only person I saw drink the stuff."

"Hmmm," Mama said. She hit Shay on the arm. "I don't believe him. Do something."

Shay sighed and looked at Allen. "Would you be willing to allow one of our people from forensics to come out and look at the truck for blood?"

"You can do whatever the hell you want at this point!" Allen exploded. He sat down in his desk chair, his nostrils flaring and his jaw tightening as he gritted his teeth. "If it means I can finally get these three out of my hair, then fine. I got enough on my plate, and I don't need to add this, too. Between this place failing, Ashley's business, my in-laws losing their house, and helping to plan Gary's funeral, I…"

Allen slouched down and put his head in his hands, clearly at his breaking point. He closed his eyes and took deep breaths. His foot tapped as he tried to calm down. After a few tense minutes, he looked at us and said, "Do whatever you want. Just…do whatever you want."

Shay looked at him with compassion. One man looking at another and understanding how it felt to have the weight of the world on your shoulders.

"Well, thank you for your time. We'll leave and let you get back to—"

"Your in-laws are losing their house?" Mama asked, cutting Shay off.

"Yeah," Allen said, not understanding why Mama was asking the question.

"Why?" Mama asked.

"Ms. Maven, why don't we leave and let Allen get back to work?" Shay asked in a gentle voice.

Mama flicked a hand at him, brushing him off. "When did your in-laws lose their house?"

"And she continues," Shay said in a low voice, looking away.

"They got the notice last week," Allen said.

"They couldn't afford to pay the mortgage?" Mama asked, tilting her head, thoughts racing through her mind.

"No, they could," Allen said. "Well, it's complicated. They lived there for thirty years, and the house was paid off, but they took out a double mortgage on it."

"Why the heck would they do something like that?" Mama asked in horror.

"The first mortgage was to help Gary out. The tow truck company hasn't been doing the best since Gary's father handed it over to him, and it needed an influx of money to help the company stay afloat. Gary also decided to open the mobile carwash business, which also needed money."

"If Gary wasn't doing good with the first business, why would his parents give him money for a second?" Mama asked.

Allen blew out a breath and shifted in his seat. "Gary is a dreamer, and his parents know that. Plus, it's not like he's bad at business. The tow truck company lost several contracts in the first few months after Gary took over, which means that people have to call us to get a tow instead of a third party calling us for business."

"Hmmm," Mama said, a thoughtful look on her face.

"And the second mortgage went to the mobile car wash?" I asked.

Allen shook his head no. "It went to Ashley."

"Your wife?" Mama asked in surprise. "They gave her money to what? Open the bed and breakfast?"

"Yes," Allen said. "They wanted to be equally supportive of her as they were to Gary."

"Then what happened?" Shay asked.

"None of the businesses are making money like they should," Allen said, rubbing his hands up and down his thighs in agitation. "Gary and Ashley were supposed to pay their parents back, but they weren't. The bed and breakfast took longer than expected to open, and then that William guy..." Allen shrugged. "My in-laws are in their mid-sixties. They didn't expect to start over at this age."

"So your in-laws told you, Gary, and Ashley last week?" Shay asked.

"No, they told Gary, and he told me," Allen said. "They're trying to keep it from Ashley because she would take it too hard."

"Huh," Shay said. "And you're sure Ashley didn't know?"

"Yes," Allen said, annoyance on his face. "She would have told me."

"Okay," Shay said, nodding his head. "Well, once again, thank you for your time."

"But I have more questions—" Mama said.

"We're leaving!" Shay said in a loud voice and gestured towards the door.

Mama sighed, and we walked out of the office and down the steps.

"I had more questions," Mama complained.

"Don't y'all go back in there," Shay said to us. "I'm serious. Cookie?"

"Understood," I said.

"Alexandra?" Shay said.

"I won't," Alexandra said, holding up a hand. "Promise."

"Ms. Maven?" Shay said.

"Hmmm," Mama said, turning her head away and her pursing her lips.

"Ms. Maven?" Shay said again.

Mama looked at him in irritation. "You are the age of my children. I am not about to stand here and answer to you. Goodbye, Shay. Come on, girls."

"You called me!" Shay yelled at us.

"I said goodbye, Shay," Mama snapped, not looking back.

We got to our car, and I looked at her over the roof of the car.

"Are we going where I think we're going?" I asked.

"Oh, you know it," Mama said.

Chapter Eleven

We stood in front of the bed and breakfast and looked up at it. It really was a beautiful five-bedroom house with a large, wrap-around porch with several rocking chairs and tables on it. Painted a bright white with a black roof, the trees surrounding the house almost touched the house, making it feel picturesque and almost like a fairytale. Looking around at the gorgeous fields of grass and the lake that wasn't too far away, I could imagine it being a great spot for a wedding.

"You don't really think that Ashley is capable of murder, do you?" Alexandra asked. She played with her necklace and looked at the house with worry.

"I think anyone is capable of anything," Mama said and then looked at me and smiled. "Except my babies."

"Thank you, Mama," I said, smiling.

"But I mean, you never know," Mama said, turning away.

"I keep a good eye on you, too, Mama," I said, not feeling offended at all.

"Gary finding out about his parents losing their house would have definitely made him angry and want to get revenge on William," Mama said. "That's why he was fussing with him at the church and trying to take their cars. But I don't think he killed William."

"Why not?" Alexandra asked. "What Allen said just adds more reason why we should think that Gary is the killer."

"I would agree, except that he went to tow their cars," Mama said.

"So?" Alexandra asked.

"If you had all this animosity and anger toward somebody, and then you got the chance to kill them, would you still keep going and tow their cars?" I asked. "Or would you run away and try to hide, so the police don't catch you?"

Alexandra paused. "Ohhh," she said, getting it. "That's a good point. Gary wouldn't have gone to Faith and William's house."

"Exactly," Mama and I said at the same time.

"And we don't think Khalil did it," I said. "So, that leaves Ashley."

"She had to have found out about her parents losing their house somehow," Mama said. "William was charging her all this money, and she blamed him for not being able to pay them back."

"And she killed him," I said.

"That's horrible and sad," Alexandra said.

"Mmm-hmm," Mama said. "Let's go and see if we can get her to talk to us."

We walked up the steps and knocked on the door. Jessica opened the door and smiled at us.

"Hello!" she said. "Welcome back. Please come in."

We walked into the house and stopped in the foyer.

"What brings you back?" Jessica asked.

"Well, actually, we wanted to look around some more," Mama said. "Alexandra is my future daughter-in-law, and when we were here the last time, we thought this might be a good spot for her to get married."

"Really?" Jessica asked with an excited voice.

"I-I-I guess so," Alexandra said, nodding her head with a stunned look on her face.

"What time of the year were you thinking?" Jessica asked her.

"I-I…you know what? I'm open to anything," Alexandra said with an awkward laugh. "The engagement is so new that I haven't really had time to process it."

"Well, that's perfect," Jessica said, walking behind the counter. She tapped a few keys on the computer and said, "We have a lot of openings right now. I would personally recommend a spring or fall wedding. Those times of the year are absolutely gorgeous, but it's really up to you and what you like."

"Um…fall?" Alexandra said, leaning on the counter. "Let's try the fall."

I looked at the computer screen and frowned. The word cancel was next to several bookings.

"Y'all have a lot of cancellations," I commented.

Jessica blushed and looked at us in embarrassment. "Unfortunately, yes. A lot of people have canceled over the last couple of weeks, or we have had to rebook people because of the repairs that were being done."

"That's tough," Mama said. "I know how hard it can be to start a new business."

"Yes, but Ashley has it under control," Jessica said. "It's just a bump in the road."

"Mm-hmm," Mama said. She looked around. "Where is Ashley?"

"She's at the funeral home with her mother, planning Gary's service," Jessica said. "But I know everything about the house, and I can help you plan a beautiful wedding. Let me show you around."

For the next twenty minutes, Jessica walked us around the house, talking about the house's history, the great features it had, and the different packages they offered.

"And this is the master bedroom," Jessica said, opening the double door with a flourish. "This is where you and your bridesmaids can get ready, and if you and your husband decide to stay, this would be your honeymoon suite."

We looked around the bedroom, feeling impressed. It was tastefully decorated with a huge king-sized bed and a small balcony that showed off the lake in the distance. Mama, Alexandra, and I split up, each looking at a different part of the room. Mama went to the bathroom while Alexandra stood on the balcony.

I walked to the side table and brushed my fingers across the wood. I looked at Jessica.

"What wonderful furniture," I said. "It's luxurious."

Jessica's smile widened. "Ashley choose well. She wanted all the guests who come to the bed and breakfast to feel like they've gone to one of the top inns in the country. It might be a bit more money, but it is well worth the cost."

"Yeah, I—" I stopped when I spotted a string on the floor. I bent down and picked it up. Frowning, I looked at her and held it up. "Looks like the floor needs another vacuuming."

"Oh, no," Jessica said, panic on her face. "I'll take that. I'm so sorry about that. I can't believe that happened."

I rubbed my thumb over the long string before handing it to her. "A hair tie, right?"

"Mmmm?" Jessica said as she balled up the string and held it tightly in her hand.

I pointed to her hand. "It's a hair tie. My brother Marques uses the same kind to tie back his dreads. William had dreads, too, right?"

Jessica nodded her head. "Right. It must have been William's. He has done work in here. It must have fallen off at some point, and I missed it when I was cleaning the room."

"This certainly would be a lovely honeymoon suite," Mama said, coming back into the room. Alexandra opened the balcony door and walked back in.

"I have to agree," I said. "This place is perfection."

I went to the bed to sit down and test it. I bounced on it several times to feel its firmness.

"I have to say that this is a nice place—Ohhh!" I said as I crashed to the floor.

"Oh, my God," Mama said, rushing to my side.

"Are you okay?" Alexandra asked, bending down to my side.

"I'm okay," I said, feeling embarrassed and in pain.

I lifted myself up and winced at the pain in my wrist. I had landed hard on it when the bed broke, and I fell slash rolled onto the floor. Shifting on the floor, I held my wrist and looked at the bed. It was completely broken on one side and leaning at a slant.

"I am so sorry," Jessica said, putting a hand to her chest. "I can't believe that happened. I don't know—"

"What happened?" Ashley asked, running into the room with a concerned look on her face. She looked around. "I heard a crash."

"The bed broke," Jessica said, pointing a hand at it.

"Not another one," Ashley moaned in despair, looking at the bed.

"Another one? What kinda place are y'all running around here?" I asked her, still holding my wrist.

"I'm very sorry," Ashley said. "We've been having issues with the beds. There's a manufacturing problem. I've already called the company."

"Call them again!" I said. (Is that a cut on my leg?) "Thank the Lord I wasn't here for real."

"It's being taken care of," Ashley said. "What are y'all doing back here?

"They wcrc here to look at the property," Jessica said. She pointed a hand at Alexandra. "She's planning her wedding."

"Apparently, I'm getting married," Alexandra said.

"What?" Ashely asked.

Alexandra shook her head. "Nothing. The engagement is so new that it's still hard for me to believe it."

"Well…congratulations," Ashley said, not sounding very sincere. She rubbed her head, and her mouth tightened. "Jessica, can you finish showing the ladies around? I need to go to the kitchen to get some aspirin."

She left the room, and Jessica gave us an unsure look before giving us a strained smile.

"I would love to continue the tour if y'all want to?" Jessica said. "Or maybe y'all would like something to drink and relax for a bit?"

"Something to drink would be lovely," Mama said. "It should have come from the owner, but I'm glad you offered."

"You'll have to excuse Ashley. She's under a lot of strain," Jessica said.

"Hmmm," Mama said.

We left the room and went to the living room. Jessica left and came back with a tray full of colorful glasses filled with lemonade. She set the tray down on the table and handed each of us a glass before sitting down.

"So, tell me about your fiancée," Jessica said, smiling at Alexandra before taking a small sip from her glass.

"Mmm?" Alexandra said. Her eyes were big as she sipped from her glass. "My fiancée? He's, um, he is…"

"A great catch," Mama said, smiling. "Go on, Alexandra. Tell her how y'all met."

"Well, we, um," Alexandra said and started telling the story of how she and Ren met.

I leaned over to Mama and whispered, "I'm going to go see if I can get some ice for my wrist."

She gave me a worried look. "Is it that bad?"

"It's stinging," I admitted.

"Do you want me to go with you?" Mama asked.

"No," I replied. "I'll be fine. Plus, I'll be back in a minute."

I got up from the couch and slipped out of the room. The kitchen was toward the back of the house, past the dining room. I opened the door and found Ashley sitting at the breakfast nook, silently crying. She looked up at me and hurriedly wiped her tears.

"Sorry," I said. "I didn't mean to disturb you. I just wanted some ice for my wrist."

"No, no, it's fine," Ashley said, dabbing her nose with her sleeve as she slid out of the booth. "I should have offered you some ice for your wrist when we were upstairs. I apologize."

"No problem," I said as I watched her pull out a Ziploc bag and fill it with ice. "You have a lot on your mind."

She grabbed a towel and put the Ziploc bag in it. Twisting it together, she said, "Here you go."

"Thanks," I said, taking it. I placed it against my wrist and winced at the cold sensation. I looked at Ashley and said, "You know, despite the bed breaking, you really do have a beautiful place."

I looked around the kitchen. While the rest of the house felt more modern and updated, the kitchen was the only area that had yet to be worked on and still retained some of its charm from the past. It was a large kitchen with white cabinets that lined the walls, a farm-style sink that sat in front of a window with billowy curtains, and white and black linoleum tiles decorated the floor. Appliances that had seen better days were nestled in the kitchen. Age and rust stains were evident despite whoever's attempt to get rid of them.

"Thank you," she said. She looked around the kitchen with sad eyes. "Although, I regret buying it."

"Why?"

"It's been nothing but a money pit," she said. She shook her head and crossed her arms. "I don't know why I thought I could do this. It was a horrible mistake."

"No, it wasn't," I said. "It's a nice place, and I'm sure it will start making money soon."

"I won't know," she said. She looked at me and gave me a watery smile. "I'm selling it."

"Really? Why?" I asked, surprised.

She shook her head and shrugged. "To stop a foolish dream? To try and get some money back? To try and help my parents? Pick a reason."

"Why do your parents need help?"

"They sunk a lot of money into this, and now they're losing their house," she said, her lips tightening. A tear slipped down her cheek, and she wiped it away. "The least I can do is make sure they don't lose their house."

"Wow," I said. "That's both kind and sweet. I'm sorry that you're losing your business."

She waved a hand, dismissing the apology. "Don't be," she said. "Like I said, it was foolish."

"And I'm sorry that your parents are losing their house. I know that can be devastating. Gary and your husband must have been very upset," I said.

She shook her head, distracted. "Gary didn't know, and I haven't told my husband yet. I found out last week."

I opened my mouth and then closed it. I wasn't sure how I was going to bring up William and the fact that I thought she was a murderer.

"Did William…charging you a lot have anything to do with this?" I asked slowly.

She gave an exasperated look. "Really? Did y'all come here to look at the place or investigate?"

"We can do two things at once," I said. "And I didn't mean to bring up a sore subject. It came up while we were investigating. So...did it?"

"Yes," she said. "If you must know, yes, it did. There were so many problems with the house that all of my money went into it. I wasn't able to pay my parents back. They're the ones who loaned me the money for the house."

"And this made you...angry?" I asked, my voice ending on an unnatural high note.

Ashley looked at me with disdain. "Are you trying to imply that I killed William?"

I sputtered and let out an awkward laugh. "Did I say that? Did you hear those words come out of my mouth? Why would I even *say* something like that?"

I turned my head away and rubbed the ice over my swollen wrist.

"Did you?" I asked in a soft voice.

"Oh, my God," Ashley said in disgust. "Get out."

"Now, hold on," I said as I watched her walk to the kitchen table. "I'm not *accusing* you of murder—"

"Oh, you're not?" Ashley said in mock surprise. She grabbed a plastic cup from the table and took a big gulp of water before sitting down. "I don't have time for this. Why don't you leave before I call the police?"

"I think you should be more concerned about me calling the police on you," I said. Ashley gave me an ugly look, and I backed up a step. "I'm just playin'! You don't know how to take a joke!"

"No, I don't," Ashley said, her eyes flashing with anger.

"Okay," I said, holding up a hand. "Listen, I'm not accusing you of murder…it's just that…well, you and your brother had a lot of reasons to kill William."

"We didn't!" Ashley snapped, her hand slamming against the table.

"Okay," I said, trying to calm her down. "I believe you. Good Lord, calm down. Why don't you tell me your side?"

"There is no side," Ashley said, shaking her head. "I hired him, and I fired him."

"Because…?"

"I couldn't afford him," Ashley said. She waved a hand around the kitchen. "There were so many problems with the house that I couldn't afford all the repairs. I told him that, unfortunately, I would have to fire him for the moment because I didn't have the money to keep up with everything."

I walked to the table and sat down.

"How did he take it?" I asked.

She shrugged. "Fine," Ashley said. "He didn't seem upset. William said he understood and that I could call him whenever I needed him. I thanked him, and he left."

"Do you think he was cheating you?" I asked.

"I…I don't know," Ashley said, looking out the window. She turned to me. "He seemed like a decent guy."

"Your brother and your husband thought otherwise," I said.

Ashley smiled and rubbed a hand over the table. "Yeah," she said softly. She sighed. "I don't know. When I first decided to buy the house, it had to be inspected. The guy who did it commented on what good shape the house was in, considering how old it was. I remember thinking how lucky I was, but when all the problems started happening, I figured it was just a matter of time."

"A matter of time?" I asked, confused.

Ashley nodded. "I knew it was too good to be true. I got the house for thirty less than the asking price because the owners wanted to move, and it wasn't selling."

"Wow, that was a bargain," I said.

"It was," Ashley agreed. "It was great because between the bank loan and the second mortgage my parents took out, I had the exact amount the house owners were asking for initially. When they agreed to sell me the house for less than the asking price, it meant that I could keep the thirty thousand and use it as start-up money for the bed and breakfast. But all the money I saved on buying the house was quickly spent."

"Whew!" I said, a big breath releasing from my body as I collapsed against the booth. "William took thirty thousand dollars from you? For repairs?"

"No," Ashley said, shaking her head. "He took about ten, and twenty thousand went to furnishing the house and replacing things."

"Twenty thousand?" I said in disbelief. "Oh, Ashley, you need to come with Mama and me and go shopping. You don't know how to bargain hunt."

A small smile appeared on Ashley's lips. "I know how to shop," she said. "But I wanted the best for the bed and breakfast. Good accommodations are what keep people coming back. Let's face it, you can only spin this town as charming so many times."

"True," I said, nodding my head. "But I don't get it. What are you spending your money on?"

"Everything," Ashley said. "Anything."

"That's true," I agreed.

"I needed to make sure that when people came to this place, they remembered it as great even if they weren't that fond of the town," Ashley said. She sighed and shook her head. "But that didn't work."

"So, there was nothing suspicious going on with William?" I asked. "Maybe somebody came by? Or you overheard him make a phone call?"

"No," Ashley said, shaking her head. "He was professional when he was here. Very nice."

"And there's no way that Allen or Gary…?" I said slowly.

"No," Ashley said in a firm voice. "They were upset, but my brother and my husband aren't murderers. They aren't that type of men."

"And what about Gary?" I asked. "Nothing comes to mind when you think about what happened to him? Anybody angry with him lately?"

"No," Ashley said. She rested her elbows on the table and leaned forward, her eyes earnest. "I know you want to find my brother's killer, but the police already did. You're just going to have to face facts. She's guilty. She killed my brother."

I sighed and looked away. I didn't believe for a minute that Faith killed Gary, but there was no convincing Ashley of that, and it didn't seem like she had any information about what could have happened to Gary or William.

"Okay," I said, feeling defeated. "Thank you for answering my questions."

Ashley nodded her head. I got up from the table and looked around the room. Spotting a trash can, I walked over to it and lifted the lid to throw away the bag of ice. I frowned when I spotted shards of blue, yellow, and pink glass in the can. It looked like the same design as the glasses that Jessica had handed us.

"Is that glass?" I asked, looking at Ashley.

"Mmm?" Ashley said, distracted. "Oh, yeah. Some of the glasses broke in the dishwasher."

"That's a lot of glass," I said.

"We've been having problems with the dishwasher," Ashley said. "I was supposed to buy a new one, but now that's the next owner's problem."

"Hmmm," I said, letting the lid fall close, a bad feeling in my stomach.

*****

"God bless, Jessica, but she has to be the most boring human being on the face of the planet," Mama said as she unlocked the door to the agency and pushed it open. "I've had more fun watching possums fight over a piece of cheese."

"She wasn't that bad," Alexandra said.

"Don't lie for that girl," Mama said, shaking her head in wonder. "All that prettiness wasted. Good Lord."

"Well, I guess it's over," I said, throwing my purse on my desk. "Khalil and Faith are going to jail for crimes they didn't commit."

"There has to be something we can do," Mama said, dropping her purse on her desk. "We can't give up on those two."

"I'm not sure what we can do," Alexandra said. "We've looked into everything, and there are no other clues."

"That doesn't mean it's over," Mama said. "It just means that it's going to be a little bit more complicated."

Mama walked behind her desk and sat down. She looked at me.

"Are you sure Ashley didn't say anything that could lead us to William's murderer?" Mama asked.

"No," I said, shaking my head. "She was adamant that he was a nice guy. Ashley didn't even want to believe that he was cheating her out of money. She said that her husband and Gary were the ones convinced that he was conning her, and she doesn't for a minute think they are capable of killing William."

"Did she say anything about Khalil?" Mama asked.

"No, but she didn't mention him when I asked if William was having any problems," I said. "I'm sure she knows he's in jail and she would have said something."

Mama sighed and leaned back in her desk chair, a hand covering her mouth as she thought.

"There has to be something," she mumbled.

I waved a hand and leaned against my desk. "Well, this whole thing is about to be a thing of the past. Ashley is selling the bed and breakfast."

"To who?" Mama asked, frowning.

"I don't know," I said.

"That's kind of abrupt, isn't it?" Alexandra asked, looking up at me from one of the chairs in front of my desk.

"Ashley said she was trying to regroup some of the money her parents put into the bed and breakfast. She's hoping to save their house," I said.

"That part bothers me," Mama said, slowly moving back and forth in her chair.

"What?" Alexandra asked.

"The fact that Ashley knew about her parents losing their house and didn't say anything," Mama said.

I shrugged. "What's the big deal? A holiday was coming up. She probably didn't want to spoil the mood."

"But not to say anything to anybody?" Mama said. She shook her head. "Uh-uh. I can maybe understand not saying something to your brother, but not to the man you lay your head next to every night?"

"Maybe Ashley thought she was saving him?" Alexandra said. "Or maybe she was stopping an argument? Allen doesn't exactly look like the type to be all warm and cuddly if she told him that she was selling a house that she had bought a few months earlier."

"I do not want to be there for that fuss," I said. I looked at Mama. "You think Ashley is hiding something by not telling anyone that she knew her parents were losing their house?"

"I don't know," Mama said softly. "Hmmm."

"Don't hmmm!" I said. "Hmmms are bad, Mama!"

"Stop that," she said and got up. "Let's go."

"Go where?" Alexandra asked, quickly grabbing her bag.

"We need to figure out why Ashley doesn't want anyone to know that she knows about the you-know-what," Mama said, pushing open the front door.

I stopped in my tracks and looked at Alexandra. "Did you get that?"

"I don't get a lot of things that your mother says," Alexandra said and walked out the door.

Chapter Twelve

"We brought doughnuts!" Mama said in a cheery voice.

"God, not today," Allen said, dropping his head against a filing cabinet. He looked up and stared at us. "Do y'all enjoy ruining people's day?"

"Ouch, and amen!" Mama said, her smile not dropping. She walked into the small office and put the box of doughnuts on Allen's desk. She tapped the lid. "We didn't buy enough for everyone. So, the first three people who get here…yeah. Anyway! We wanted to come by and give you a little peace offering."

"Your disappearance would have been peace enough," Allen said as he sat down in his chair.

Mama's smile cracked at the edges. "You're not going to tell me off and take my doughnuts. Choose one."

"Ah, there it is," Allen said, pointing at her faltering smile. He sat back in his chair. "What y'all want?"

"I was gonna try to save your feelings, but you keep letting the devil win in this battle. Alright, then. Who is your wife selling the bed and breakfast to?" Mama asked.

Allen's head drew back, and he scoffed. "Ashley's not selling the bed and breakfast."

"Ohhh, seems like you don't know what's going on in yo' house, huh?" Mama said, beaming again. "Wonder what else is going on that you don't know about. Imma put it out there and let it go."

"Hey…!" Allen barked.

"Hey, you called her that kind of woman. I didn't," Mama said, putting a hand to her chest. "If that's the first thing that came to your mind, then maybe you need to have a discussion with your wife."

"Are you done?" Allen asked, glowering at her.

"Hey, I came in looking for peace. You're the one who invited the devil in like a vampire in the night. That heartache is on you," Mama said. "Now, tell me the buyers."

"There are no buyers," Allen said. "Ashley isn't selling the bed and breakfast. Where did you hear that?"

"Ashley," I said.

"Excuse me?" Allen said, looking stunned.

I nodded my head. "We talked to her less than an hour ago. According to her, she's selling the bed and breakfast to try and help her parents save their house. She knows that they are losing it."

"What?" Allen said, shocked.

"She learned about it last week," Mama said. She drew a circle on the doughnut box and said, "And clearly didn't tell you from the look on your face."

Allen cursed. He closed his eyes and started tapping a pen on the desk.

"She wasn't supposed to find out," he said.

"You were going to keep something like that from her?!" Mama asked in disbelief, her eyebrows raising. "Tell me if I'm wrong, but I saw a grown woman less than an hour ago!"

"I didn't mean it like that," Allen said. "I…we were going to tell her, but later! After we had fixed everything!"

"Is she that delicate?" I asked. "Because she doesn't need to be by herself if she's that delicate."

"It's not like that," Allen said. "Ashley takes everything to heart. Her parents were afraid that if she found out about them losing their house, she would blame herself, and they wanted to avoid that."

"By not telling her?" Mama asked.

"Yes," Allen said. "Gary found out and told me because he thought we could work overtime to get back some of the contracts we lost and make more money. Once we got everything settled, we would tell Ashley. Now, she's gone and done something foolish like this. Ugh!"

Mama looked at him and then slid the box of doughnuts across the desk.

"Here, have a doughnut. You'll feel better," she said. She sighed and slid her purse strap down as she pulled out a chair and sat down. "Listen, it's clear that you love your wife and want what's best for her. So, try and think. Your wife finds out that her parents are losing their home and decides to sell her bed and breakfast. This all happens within a week. Who would be willing to buy her bed and breakfast that quick?"

"Mmm…Kirk and Sharon Nelson?" he said with a shrug. "Maybe? They tried to buy the house before Ashley, but the owners took a liking to Ashley and decided to sell to her. The wife liked the idea of her being a young entrepreneur."

"Kirk and Sharon Nelson," Mama said. "Where have I heard those names before?"

*****

"It smells like sh-"

"Cookie!" Mama snapped, giving me a look.

I covered my nose and tried to breathe through my mouth. (That didn't work. It still smelled like sh-)

"Welcome to Kirk and Sharon Nelson's Rescue Bird Mission!" Sharon Nelson said, smiling at us. She was of average height with a little weight to her, and a mass of blond curls on her head was covered with a hat to block out the sun. Her skin was tanned from working out in the sun, and she wore a pink floral shirt and old jeans that had been cut off at the knees to form shorts.

"Please, come in!" Sharon said, waving a hand at us.

We walked into the building. It was a mixture of indoor and outdoor settings with flowers, man-made streams, and signs that talked about all the different birds that the rescue mission had.

"We aim to help the natural bird populations in our area by rescuing them, rehabilitating them, and then reintroducing them to the wild-"

"I'm sorry," I said, interrupting her. I waved the hand that wasn't covering my nose. "There's just such an…*interesting* smell in here. What is it?"

"Oh! We like to make sure that all the things we use are natural and locally sourced. We mix our soil on the grounds from local farm's droppings and leftover food peels," Sharon said, smiling. "It makes the best soil for the flowers."

"Oh, does it?" I said, chuckling. I looked at Mama. "I'll be in the car."

Mama gripped my arm, her nails biting into my flesh.

"Stay, Cookie. You don't want to miss the lesson on the different birds," Mama said.

"I'm sure I'll be okay," I said. "Release me, woman."

"Is that a—" Alexandra walked away with Sharon, pointing at a poster about a specific bird.

"If I have to suffer through this horrific smell, so do you," Mama said.

"Parents are supposed to want better for their children. Why don't you?" I asked, pulling away from her.

"Because someday I'm going to tell this story, and I need your co-sign on how bad it was. Now, be quiet and sleuth," Mama said.

We walked back to Sharon in time to hear her say, "We also sell our special soil mix. You can purchase it—"

"Good God, no!" Mama shouted. Sharon looked at her and blinked. Mama pinched her nose and tried to regroup. "Um, uh…I meant…I meant, no…I get mine from a local guy who is a close friend of the family and…and I….you know….I don't want to turn my back on him."

I looked at her. "Well, I don't feel embarrassed."

"Sharon? Have you seen my—" A tall man walked around the corner and stopped when he saw us. "Oh, sorry! I didn't realize you were with visitors!"

"Oh, no problem," Sharon said, waving him over. "This is my husband, Kirk."

He walked over to Sharon and put his arm around her. She looked up at him adoringly.

"Hi, folks," he said with a goofy grin, raising a hand. "Hope you all are having a good time."

"Great so far," Alexandra said, nodding her head.

Mama stared at her while I slowly shook my head and kept my hand over my nose.

"So…" Mama said, looking at Sharon and Kirk. "What made you two start a bird rescue mission?"

"Geez, it had to be forty years ago when we first met. I've always loved birds, and Kirk has always rescued animals. It just seemed like the perfect way to put our passions together," Sharon said.

"And I've loved every day of it," Kirk said, smiling down at Sharon.

"They're the killers. No one is that much in love," I whispered to Mama. She elbowed me in the ribs.

"What?" Sharon asked, looking at me.

"I asked, do you live on the grounds? You two seem so dedicated to the birds," I said. "The loud, squawking birds."

"No. We live about ten minutes away in a little house. It's close enough to be here in case of an emergency," Kirk said.

"Oh, that's wonderful," Mama said. "Do you like living there?"

"Yes," Sharon said, nodding her head.

"Really? Never thought about living anywhere else?" Mama asked.

"No," Sharon said, hesitancy in her voice. She looked up at Kirk and then back at Mama. "Why?"

"Oh, you never know," Mama said, shrugging. "I thought maybe a darling five-bedroom house might have been something of interest."

"Are you talking about that house on River Road?" Kirk asked.

"Oh, have you been?" Mama asked.

"Yes," Sharon said. "We put in an offer for it. We wanted to buy it for our son and daughter-in-law."

(Squawking birds and smelly poop are that lucrative?)

"They're coming back, and they have four children. We thought it would be a great welcome home gift," Kirk explained.

(Why can't I get those types of welcome home gifts?)

"Welcome home gift? Well, damn, we might need to become friends," Mama said. She caught herself and shook her head to clear it. "I mean, losing out on that house must have been upsetting."

"Yes, but we were able to find something else for them and our grandkids," Sharon said. "Plus, I like the idea of it being turned into a bed and breakfast. I think it's charming. Too bad they couldn't rebook us."

"Rebook?" I asked. "What do you mean?"

"We called when it first opened to book a reservation. A little weekend getaway before the kids and the grandkids came back," Sharon said, smiling up at Kirk. She looked at me. "But they called us back and said they had to cancel our reservation unfortunately because of unexpected repairs. I called back a few weeks later to see if maybe they could rebook us, but the woman said they were booked until December."

She shrugged. "I guess I waited too long. I knew that bed and breakfast would be popular."

*****

Our heads slowly rose, and we looked into the kitchen window.

"I don't feel right about this," Alexandra whispered. She sounded extra loud because of the quietness of the night.

"About what?" Mama whispered, her eyes scanning for movement.

"About breaking into here!" Alexandra said, looking at Mama. "Wouldn't it be better if we brought our concerns to Shay, and he went through the proper channels to get a search warrant?"

Mama and I looked at her.

"That was adorable," Mama said. "Cookie, open the door."

Staying low, I duck-walked over to the door, pulled out my lockpicking kit from my purse, and started working. A few moves to the left and a few turns to the right, and the door swung open. We hurried into the house, and I closed the door behind us. Turning on the lights on our phones, we began to search.

"What exactly are we looking for?" Alexandra asked, quickly opening a kitchen drawer and closing it.

"Anything and everything," Mama said, opening a cabinet. "There's something wrong with Ashley and this house. Everybody in this case is somehow connected to this house. There has to be something here."

"Maybe Ashley just has a case of really bad luck?" I suggested, closing a drawer.

"I don't believe that for a minute," Mama said. "Anything?"

"No," Alexandra said, shaking her head as she stood.

"Nothing," I said, closing a drawer.

"Let's split up," Mama said. "You two take upstairs, and I'll take this floor."

"Got it," I said and rushed out of the kitchen.

Alexandra and I climbed up the stairs, and each took a bedroom. Much like the rest of the house, the bedroom I entered was painted in soft hues of white, grey, and black. I started looking around, opening the drawers on bedside tables, and looking under the bed. I sighed in disappointment and leaned on the bed to stand up. It creaked heavily under the pressure and gave a slight tremble.

"Woah!" I whispered and held my hands out as if I could magically stop the bed from doing anything else. I waited a few seconds to see if anything else would happen. Frowning, I pushed down on the bed again, and it groaned. I got on my knees and pulled up the bedding to get a better look at the bedframe. My frown deepened when I noticed several of the screws that held the bedframe together unscrewed to the point that they were barely in the holes.

"What the-?" I whispered. I sat back and let the bedding drop. My mind raced, and I went to the other side of the bed to look. The screws were perfectly drilled into place. Getting suspicious, I stood up and went to find Alexandra.

"Oh!" I said, catching myself before I bumped into her in the hallway. "Did you find anything?"

"No," she said. "Everything is empty and waiting for guests to check-in."

"Did you check the beds?" I asked.

"No," Alexandra said slowly, a confused look on her face. "I checked the drawers and the closets. Why would I check the beds?"

"I need to see something," I said, going around her and walking into one of the bedrooms. I lifted the bedding and looked at the screws. They were perfectly screwed into the bedframe, nice and tight.

"Huh," I said, letting the bedding drop.

"What?" Alexandra asked, shining her phone at me. "Did you expect to find something?"

"The bedframe in the other bedroom," I said. "The screws are completely loose in the frame. It almost broke when I used it to lift myself up."

"Didn't Jessica say they were having manufacturing problems with the beds?" Alexandra asked. "That one is probably broken like the one from this afternoon."

"Yeah, but it looks like someone unscrewed them just enough to make them look like they are in the bedframe but not hold the bed together, and they are unscrewed in strategic places," I said. "It was unscrewed on one side but not the other."

Alexandra shook her head in bewilderment. "Why would someone—?"

"To make someone fall and hurt themselves," I said, looking down at my wrist. "Ohhhh! I'm suing!"

"You think it's on purpose?!" Alexandra asked in shock as she followed me out of the room.

"Heck yeah, I think it's on purpose!" I said. "And I can't wait for them to hear from my lawyer!"

We walked down the stairs to find Mama standing behind the front desk, talking to someone on her phone.

"Uh-huh," Mama said, nodding her head. "Really? That's interesting. Thanks. Bye."

She hung up the phone and looked at us.

"Did you really just stand there and take a phone call in the middle of a break-in?" I asked, pointing at her phone.

"There's always time for good investigating, Cookie, and this was good investigating," Mama said, shaking the phone at me. (She meant good gossiping.)

"What did you find out?" I asked, walking closer to the desk.

"I went through the computer and noticed that one of the people who booked was a former client of mine," Mama said. She made a face. "I'm not saying that she was happy to be woken up in the middle of the night; in fact, she let me know in no uncertain terms that she was unhappy, but she was very helpful. She said that she had booked a room for her and her husband for June. You know, to spark the romance again. Even though I don't know why she is trying with that fool after he—"

"Mama, focus," I said, tapping the desk several times to get her back on track.

"Oh, right," she said with a slight shake of her head. "Well, she said that Jessica called her and told her there were several renovations being done on the house and she had to cancel her booking. It's the exact same story as the one Sharon told us."

"I don't get it," I said. "Jessica and Ashley already said that the repairs were taking more time than they thought, and it had caused a bunch of cancellations."

"True, and get this. Look at their bookings," Mama said. We hurried behind the desk and stared at the computer. "Nothing but a sea of cancellations. Not a reservation in sight."

"Why would she do that? Why would she lie?" Alexandra said. "They kept getting cancellations. They needed as many bookings as possible."

"Because Jessica is behind all the damages. That's why everything was taking so long because Jessica was breaking things on purpose to cost Ashley money and make the bed and breakfast a failure," I said. Mama smiled and nodded her head. I told her about the bed, and her smile dropped.

"Well, that is downright evil," Mama said. "What game is this girl up to?"

"Ashley said she was selling the bed and breakfast," I said. "How much do you want to bet that she is selling it to Jessica?"

"Dang," Alexandra said. "With friends like that, who needs enemies?"

"No, what Jessica needs is an ass whoppin'," Mama said, nodding her head. "Let's get out of here. We'll talk to Ashlcy in thc morning."

*****

"Good morning!" Mama said in a bright and cheery voice as she walked into the bed and breakfast.

"Good morning to you," Jessica said, pausing as she arranged flowers in a vase. "You're back."

"Absolutely," Mama said. "We had a few questions for Ashley."

"Oh?" Jessica said in surprise. "Is it something I could help you with?"

"No, I think it's best if Ashley answered these questions," Mama said. "Don't worry. You'll have time enough to do some talkin'."

Jessica laughed. "Well, okay. She's in the kitchen. You go through the dining room, and it's right there. I'll be outside if you need me."

"Okay," Mama said, watching as she walked around the desk and slipped through the front door. "Let's go, ladies."

We walked in a straight line through the house and to the kitchen. Ashley looked up from the kitchen sink where she was washing dishes. She gave us a confused look as she grabbed a dish towel and dried her hands.

"What are y'all doing here?" she asked.

"We just wanted to ask you a few more questions," Mama said. "Cookie, told me that you're selling this house?"

"Yes," Ashley said, nodding her head. "As soon as possible."

"Do you mind if I ask to whom?" Mama asked.

"I'm not sure that matters," Ashley said slowly. She looked between the three of us. "If you must know, I'm selling the house to Jessica."

"Ahh," Mama said, smiling. "And just one more question. I have a small hunch, and please tell me if I'm right. Did you tell Jessica that your parents were losing their house?"

"I…yes," Ashley said. "It was a lot to bear, and I had to tell someone."

"Why not your husband? Or your brother?" I asked.

"They would have tried to do something about it and would have excluded me," Ashley said, shaking her head. She threw the towel on the counter. "They mean well, but they act like I'm made out of glass. Like I can't handle a little bit of bad news."

"Perfect," Mama said. The sound of a car pulling up in front of the house caused Mama's smile to widen. "And more perfect. Thank you for your time, Ashley."

We left the kitchen and walked out of the house. Shay was getting out of his car and looking at us with confusion. He slammed his car door shut and walked around the front of the car.

"Y'all called me to come over here. What is this about?" he asked.

"Oh, oh, oh, hold on," I said. "I always wanted to do this."

I turned around to where Jessica was standing. "There she is, officer. Arrest her!" I said, pointing a finger at Jessica.

"It's too early in the morning for this," Shay sighed, pinching the bridge of his nose.

"What-?" Jessica said as she stood in front of the bed and breakfast. She was carrying a box full of flowers that were waiting to be planted. "What's going on?"

"Oh, don't act innocent now," I said. I wagged a finger at her. "We see through your whole game. It's over. Arrest her!"

Mama and Alexandra stood behind me, nodding their heads.

"Arrest me for what?" Jessica asked. "I haven't done anything."

"I don't get paid enough for this," Shay mumbled. "Ma'am, would you mind putting down the flowers and talking to me for a bit?"

"Talk about what?" Jessica asked, bending down to drop the box on the ground.

"Talk about your sneaky, underhanded self, for starters," Mama said. "We know you caused all the damage to this house, and may I say, shame on you!"

"I didn't do any—" Jessica protested.

"Give up! We have proof!" I said. I hit Shay on the chest with the back of my hand. "Ain't that right, Shay? Don't we have proof?"

"There's no pro—" Shay began to say, closing his eyes in frustration.

"Alright, so what?" Jessica said, dropping all pretense of niceness. "So, I played a few harmless jokes that got out of hand? It's not illegal."

"What the--? Yes, it is!" Shay said, looking at her in shock. "I was over here tryin' to defend you…it doesn't matter. It's illegal to cause property damage!"

"Ashley's not going to have me arrested. Please," Jessica scoffed.

"Woooow," I said. "You're that type of bold, huh?"

Shay rubbed a hand over his face and tried to regain control of the situation.

"Did you cause all the damage to the bed and breakfast?" he asked.

Jessica crossed her arms and lifted a shoulder. She raised a brow, daring him to challenge her.

"Oh, see, she needs to be taught a lesson," Mama said, shaking her head. "Shay? Shay, do something before I do something."

"Ms. Maven, please," Shay said, holding up his hands to calm her down.

"You're lucky I hurt my hip last week, Jessica!" Mama yelled at her.

"And that's why you'll be arrested for killing William and Gary!" I shouted.

"What is all this commotion?!" Ashley asked as she came out of the house and walked down the steps. She looked around the neighborhood, embarrassment on her face. She crossed her arms over her silk blouse and looked at us. "Can y'all please let me save the little bit of dignity I have left?"

"No, because Jessica is the one who has been sabotaging your bed and breakfast," Mama said.

"*What?!*" Ashley said, her head snapping to Jessica.

"Mm-hmm, that's right, girl," I said, slipping to Ashley's side. I leaned in close. "She's the one breaking all those glasses you bought, canceling guests, and causing those beds to break. Trifflin', just trifflin'."

"You—? You….*YOU!*" Ashley screamed and then charged at Jessica like a football player. They fell to the ground with Ashley on top of her, slapping at Jessica's face repeatedly.

"Oh! Oh, Lord!" Mama said, stepping back.

"Great!" Shay said, throwing up his hands before running over to the two women and attempting to break them up. "Stop! Stop! C'mon now, I'm the law! I'm tellin' you to stop!"

"Ohhh, she got her by the hair," I said, cringing and shaking my head as Ashley pulled at Jessica's hair with all her might. "And that weave looks fresh. Nice and tight. That's gonna hurt."

"*Get off of me!*" Jessica screamed, swinging wildly.

"*You no good, raggedy, trifflin' guttersnipe,*" Ashley screamed. Shay tugged hard, and Ashley lost her grip. She struggled in Shay's arms, trying to get back to Jessica. "*I picked yo' ass up from the streets, you…you…you…*"

"Brokedown, greasy potato chip bag lookin' heffa," Mama supplied. I looked at her, and Mama shrugged. "What? She needed a little help."

"Potato chip bag?" I asked.

Mama waved a hand at Jessica in frustration. "She has on the same colors as a bag of barbeque potato chips. It's the first thing that came to my mind."

"There were so many other options," I said, holding out my hands. "Crooked-eye heffa. Flat booty heffa. Look like you haven't brushed your teeth in three Mondays heffa. Why potato chip bag?"

"Uh-uh," Mama said, shaking her head. "She a lowdown criminal, but she's pretty. I can't take that from her. She wasted that pretty on this town."

"Okay, okay! That's enough!" Shay said in a loud, commanding voice. He put Ashley down. She was breathing hard, still staring daggers at Jessica as she fixed her clothes.

"She attacked me! I want her arrested!" Jessica demanded, pointing a finger at Ashley.

"Oh, you want me arrested, do you? I'm gonna give you a reason to have me arrested!" Ashley went for her again.

"No," Shay said, stopping Ashley in her tracks, causing her to stumble. He looked at Jessica. "Now, I can't stop you if you want to press charges, but I would think hard and long about what you've done before you open the door to people getting arrested."

"Do you know how much money I spent on this place?!" Ashley shouted. "My *parents* are losing their house because of you!"

"No, they're losing their house because of *you!*" Jessica accused.

"Oh, that's it! I want her arrested!" Ashley said to Shay as she pointed at Jessica.

"If I'm getting arrested, then she needs to be arrested, too!" Jessica said, looking at Shay.

"Oh, Lord," Shay sighed, looking away in frustration.

"Well, this is a hot mess," Mama said.

*****

Mama, Alexandra, and I sat in the police station waiting for Shay, or anybody, to come and tell us what was going on. After Jessica and Ashley demanded that each other get arrested, Shay called for two officers to come and pick them up and then followed them to the station to talk to Jessica. It had been hours, and we were still waiting for any news.

"It has to be Jessica," I said for the umpteenth time. "It makes sense. She wanted to get the bed and breakfast from Ashley, so she sabotaged the house and killed William and Gary."

"But why and how?" Alexandra asked.

"I don't have that figured out yet, but out of everybody involved, she has to be the murderer," Mama said.

"Maybe not," Shay said as he walked toward us.

"What? What do you mean?" Mama asked, jumping.

"Sorry, Ms. Maven, but Jessica has an alibi that checks out," Shay said.

The three of us groaned in disappointment.

"What is it?" Mama asked.

"She drove two hours away to go to service with her grandma and then serve food to the homeless," Shay said. "I talked to the pastor myself, and he confirmed that she was there the whole time."

"Unbelievable!" I said. "So, she gets away with doing all those things to Ashley?"

"No," Shay said. "Ashley and Jessica were both booked for what they did, but they'll be out in about an hour or two. Depending on how much damage she did, Jessica will most likely be ordered to pay it back by a judge."

"This is…" Mama's mouth tightened, and she shook her head.

"What about Faith and Khalil?" I asked, rubbing my head. (I felt a headache coming on.)

"They are still arrested and will be prosecuted for the murders they did," Shay said.

"They're innocent!" I said.

"That's not what the evidence says, Cookie," Shay said. He shrugged and started to walk backward. "Sorry."

I watched as he walked away, my heart slowly sinking to the ground.

"We have to do something," I said. "We can't let Faith and Khalil be blamed for something they didn't do."

"We'll figure out something," Mama said. Her foot started tapping, and her face scrunched as she thought. "Shay said Jessica would be out in an hour or two, right?"

"Yeah," Alexandra said.

Mama looked at me. "How fast can you look up an address?"

"How fast can you gossip?" I countered, each of us pulling out our phones.

*****

"It's broad daylight, and you're breaking into her apartment!" Alexandra hissed.

"Desperate times call for desperate measures. Now, move over here, so no one sees what we're doing," Mama said and then physically moved Alexandra over a few steps to better hide us.

"This is a bad idea," Alexandra said, shaking her head.

"Mm-hmm, and I'll tell the police you had nothing to do with it if we get arrested," Mama said, not paying Alexandra any mind. "Cookie, do you have it?"

"Almost," I said as I tried to open the lock on the door. "I just need it to…there!"

I opened the door, and we hurried into Jessica's apartment. It was a cute place and brightly colored with the walls painted yellow and an almost bohemian vibe. Very different from what I would have imagined Jessica's place to look like. She was so put together and modelesque. I would have thought her place would be more sleek and modern, not like this.

"Look everywhere!" Mama said as she started searching, not wasting time.

"We need to find some type of evidence that proves Jessica is lying and was here," I said.

"But she wasn't, and I'm pretty sure a pastor is not going to lie about something like that," Alexandra said.

"It could be a conspiracy," Mama said.

"Ms. Maven?" Alexandra asked in confusion.

"Maybe not. Keep looking," Mama said, moving a pillow on the couch.

We spent the next twenty minutes searching through Jessica's apartment. I shut a cabinet door in

Jessica's dining room and walked a few feet to the living room.

"There's nothing, Mama. We're going to have to give up on this one."

Mama sighed and sat down on the couch in defeat. "Maybe so," she said, looking around.

"You guys?" Alexandra said, her voice shaky.

"What?" I asked with concern. I turned my head and watched as she came out of Jessica's bedroom, holding a shirt between her fingertips and far away from her body.

"I found this," she said. "Look."

The shirt was a dark blue color, and the bottom of it was even darker, appearing to be stained.

"What is that?" I asked, walking closer. "Is that…blood?"

"I think I'm going to be sick," Alexandra said, turning her head and gagging. She shook the shirt. "Take it."

I stepped back. "I don't want it!"

"Where did you find it?" Mama asked.

"At the bottom of her laundry hamper," Alexandra said.

"You went through her laundry hamper?" I asked in surprise.

"You said we were supposed to search everywhere," Alexandra said.

"Yeah, but I draw the line at dirty drawers," I said, shaking my head. "If you're a murderer and you hid something among things that have touched your intimate parts. Uh-uh, you won that round."

"Can someone please take this from me? *Please?*" Alexandra said.

Mama took the shirt between her fingertips and looked at it, slowly turning it this way and that.

"It doesn't look like blood," Mama said, frowning. "And it's way too big for Jessica. It looks like a man's shirt."

She took the shirt and brought it closer to her face, sniffing.

"Don't you dare bring that to your—" I gagged. "Oh, my God, you have whatever is on that shirt."

"Cookie, stop," Mama said. "Smell this."

"No, thank you."

"Cookie," Mama said in a firm voice.

"You taught me early in life that no means no. No, thank you," I said, standing firm.

"Cookie, come smell this."

"Uh-uh. No is an answer, too. No, thank you," I said.

"You are acting childish," Mama said.

"Okay, I'll be her. No, thank you," I said, nodding my head. I pointed at Alexandra. "Get that one to smell it."

"Please, no. I really think I'm going to vomit. I can't believe that I dug through someone's dirty laundry. I'm having flashbacks," Alexandra said.

"It smells like cranberry juice," Mama said, becoming fed up with us.

"And you needed a second opinion? You could have just told us that," I said.

"Focus, you two. Doesn't this look like the same work shirt as what Allen wore?" Mama said.

"What everybody at the tow truck company wore," Alexandra said. "Ohhh, Allen said that Gary was the only one who drank cranberry juice! Remember?"

"And that it spilled in the tow truck he had cleaned," I said. "You think this is the link between Jessica and the murders? She was there when Gary went to tow Faith and William's cars?"

"Maybe so," Mama said. "Let's bring this back to Shay."

*****

"You broke into her…why do I even try with y'all?" Shay asked.

"Boy, stop concentrating on what we did and focus on what we found," Mama said, shaking the shirt at him. "This connects Jessica to Gary's murder."

"It's something of interest, but it doesn't connect her," Shay said. "She has an alibi for the time of the murders."

"Then explain why she has this shirt," Mama said.

Shay sighed. "I can't even take this as evidence," he said.

"Do you need us to talk to her because I don't mind talking to her," Mama said.

"No, I don't need you to talk to her," Shay said. "I'll take care of it. You three wait here and *don't* break into anybody else's place. Okay?"

"I can make no promises," I said.

Shay mumbled as he walked away, and the three of us sat down on a bench to wait.

"Look. There's Allen," Alexandra said, nodding her head toward him.

He walked into the station, looking anxious and worried.

"He's probably here to pick up Ashley," Mama said. She waited a beat and then said, "Let's go talk to him."

Allen was standing at the front desk, talking to an officer, trying to figure out when Ashley was going to be released.

He took one look at us and turned away in disgust. "Good Lord, not you three. Listen, I don't have time today."

"We understand," Mama said. "We know you're here for Ashley."

"Thank you," Allen said and turned back to the desk.

"So, you really had no idea that Jessica was behind all this mess?" Mama asked.

Allen looked at her in disbelief. "What happened to you being understanding?"

"Okay, I'm sorry," Mama said, holding up a hand. Allen turned back to the desk and opened his mouth. "But it never occurred to you that Jessica might have been the one?"

Allen looked at Mama in exasperation. "No," he said in a firm voice. "If I had for a moment thought Jessica was screwing over wife, I would have fired her myself."

He turned back to the desk. "We should have never helped her."

"Yeah, Ashley mentioned that," Mama said. "Said something about finding Jessica on the streets?"

"I wouldn't say that Jessica was on the streets, but she was unemployed for several months and was doing bad financially," Allen said.

"How did Jessica get the job with Ashley?" I asked. "Were they friends before the bed and breakfast?"

"No," Allen said. He winced. "I'm afraid it was my fault. Jessica is the girlfriend of one of the guys who works for me. He told me about her situation, and I told Ashley. After interviewing her, Ashley decided to hire her."

"Who? Which employee?" Mama asked, tilting her head.

"Max Hernandez," Allen said.

"Bald-headed Max?" Mama asked.

"Yeah, his head is shaved," Allen said. "Why?"

"How long have they been dating?" I asked.

Allen shrugged. "Years?" he said. "I'm not sure."

Mama sputtered, and as one, we turned and ran out of the police station.

"Get to the car!" Mama shouted. "Call Shay on the way!"

*****

We got to the tow truck yard and parked. Getting out of the car, we ran past the gates and looked for Max.

"Hey, hey, you!" Mama said. "Young man, come over here!"

A guy in his twenties frowned and walked over to us.

"Yeah?" he asked.

"We're looking for Max Hernandez," Mama said. "Have you seen him?"

"He's out on a call," he said and walked away.

"Great!" I said, throwing my hands up in the air and feeling defeated. "Now what?"

"Maybe we can find him!" Mama said and turned toward the car.

"You want to drive around town looking for a *tow truck* ?" I asked in disbelief as I followed her. "Are you crazy? We're never going to find him!"

"It's better than sitting here and waiting for him," Mama said, slipping into the driver's seat.

"We're never going to find him," I said as she started driving.

"I have to agree with Cookie, Ms. Maven," Alexandra said. "It's liking trying to find a needle in a haystack!"

"Well, keep on looking!" Mama said. "We can't lose hope!"

"I've lost it," I said drily. "It's gone. It's outside looking for a ride. Now what?"

Mama glanced at me. "You were always a bitter child."

"Mmm," I said. My phone rang, and I reached into my purse to grab it. "Hello?"

"I would ask if y'all were at home or at y'all's agency, minding y'all's business, but I already know the answer," Shay said.

"Well, dang. Hello to you too," I said, rolling my eyes.

"Who is that?" Mama asked.

"Shay. Being sassy," I said, looking at her.

"Sassy?! Cookie, I'm a grown man. You don't describe me as sassy—!"

I pulled the phone from my ear and tapped it. "You're on speakerphone!"

Silence.

"Hello, Ms. Maven," Shay said. "Is there any way I can convince you to stop doing whatever you are doing?"

"No, but I love that you keep thinking one day I will listen to you. Keep hope alive," Mama said. "Max is the killer!"

"Okay," Shay said. "Who is Max?"

"Max Hernandez," I said. "He's one of the workers for Gary and Allen at the tow truck company. He's the boyfriend of Jessica!"

"That's how she got the job with Ashley. Ashley and Allen knew Jessica through Max," Mama said.

"Okay," Shay said slowly. "How is he the killer? I'm not seeing the connection."

"We figured it all out. Jessica came up with a plan to take the bed and breakfast from Ashley. She started breaking things and forcing Ashley to spend money with the hope that Ashley would have to close her business early because she couldn't afford to keep it open," I said.

"And with Jessica being a dear friend and there for her, Jessica was hoping that Ashley would decide to sell the house to her," Alexandra said, leaning between the seats to get closer to the phone. "And she would be able to take over the bed and breakfast. She had access to all the guests and could call them back and suddenly have open reservations for them."

"Which is exactly what happened, especially when Jessica found out that Ashley's parents were in dire circumstances and Ashley wanted to help them. I bet you Jessica applied more pressure to Ashley when she found that out," Mama said. "But something must have caused Jessica to panic."

"Like what?" Shay asked.

"We think William saw her sabotaging the house and figured out what she was doing but didn't say anything," I said. "But then Gary confronted him about cheating his sister."

"So, William was cheating Khalil out of money, but he wasn't cheating Ashley," Shay said. "He was doing honest work."

"Exactly," Mama said. "We think he went to talk to Ashley on Saturday after the confrontation with Gary, but Jessica was there and panicked. We found his hair tie in one of the bedrooms, so maybe he went there to get proof or talk to Ashley, and Jessica interrupted them? Anyway, Jessica called Max, and they came up with a plan."

"She would spend Easter with her grandma at a church and make sure that she had an alibi, and Max would take care of William. No one would suspect Max because who would think of something like this?" I said.

"Max saw William at the church, and it was sheer luck that William was by his truck, grabbing eggs for his kids," Mama said. "They talked, William walked away, and Max grabbed the wrench and followed."

"Khalil was literally in the wrong place at the wrong time," Alexandra said.

"It's a reach, but okay," Shay said. "You think this guy is only guilty for William's murder?"

"No," Mama said. "Gary was furious with William and wanted revenge. He called Max to help him tow Faith and William's cars. Gary went back to the tow truck to get the paperwork and then went back to the house to show Faith. He probably walked into the house and called out for Faith, but she was upstairs getting aspirin for her headache. Max followed Gary, grabbed a knife from the kitchen, and killed him."

"Why kill Gary?" Shay asked.

"We're…" I glanced at Mama and then said in a rush, "We're not completely sure of that part, but as soon as we confront Max, we'll be able to answer that."

"Confront…? Where are y'all?" Shay asked.

"We're looking for Max," Mama said. "He's somewhere in town on a tow."

"So, what are y'all doing?"

"We're…driving down random streets looking for him," I admitted reluctantly. "Oh! The icee place! Can we stop and get a cherry icee?!"

"A grape and orange icee does sound delicious right now," Alexandra said, staring at the building longingly.

"Cookie, concentrate!" Mama snapped. "No, we don't have time for no damn icee. We're on the trail of a murderer. What's wrong with you?!"

"It's not like we're gonna find him! We could stop for an icee!" I said, flinging my hand.

"Y'all?" Alexandra said, leaning close to the window.

"I can't believe that in the middle of a case, you are worried about an icee," Mama said in disgust.

"Ohhhh, like we don't remember the many time you have stopped for fries," I said.

"Y'all?" Alexandra said louder.

"Are y'all really fighting about an icee?" Shay asked, the sound of cars honking coming through the phone.

"It's not about the icee. It's the principle!" I shouted into the phone.

"How, Cookie? How is an icee a principle?" Mama asked.

I pointed a finger at her. "How is it okay for you to stop in the middle of a case for food but not me?" I asked.

"Because fries are energy food," Mama said. "How does that not make sense?"

My mouth dropped. (You see what I go through?)

"Y'all?!" Alexandra said.

"This don't make no sense," Shay said. "Fussin' over some icees."

I squinted my eyes at Mama and pointed a finger at her. "Listen here, woman, there will be a day when you are old and withered, and it will be hot as Marie Jenkins in a club full of men, and your old behind is going to want an icee, and you know what I'm going to do? I'm going to drive on by and let you suffer."

"Y'all! Isn't that Max?" Alexandra said, pointing at him through the window.

"*What?!*" Mama and I said at the same time. Mama hit the brakes, and we came to a hard stop. I put my hand out to brace myself, and my seatbelt pulled across my chest.

"Ouch!" I said, rubbing my chest.

"Why didn't you say something earlier?!" Mama fussed.

"I was trying to get y'all's attention!"Alexandra said.

"Girl, you need to learn how to speak up louder!" Mama said. She looked over her shoulder and then moved into the left lane before turning down a street with rows of houses.

"Where are y'all?" Shay asked, urgency in his voice.

I looked around for a sign. "Lilac Road," I said.

"I know where that is. I'm only a few minutes away," he said.

"Okay," I said and hung up the phone.

We got out of the car and slowly approached Max. He was kneeling down and securing an old gold-colored car that had seen better days to his tow truck. An older woman was standing over him and cursing him out. (I won't write what she said. No reason to dirty your soul like that.) She was wearing a lavender-colored house dress and flip-flops, and her hair, which was more grey than black, was in a haphazard ponytail.

"Y'all act like y'all don't have nothing better to do than bother folks!" the woman fussed, waving her hand at him as she stood on the sidewalk. "You should be ashamed of yourself!"

"Ma'am, I'm just doing my job," Max said calmly. He stood up and glanced at us in surprise. "Hello?"

"Hi," Mama said. "Looks like you made a new friend."

"He's no friend of mine!" the woman said, spittle flying. "He's a bald-headed bas—"

"Whew, Lord," Mama said in a low voice as the woman proceeded to curse Max out. Mama scratched the back of her neck. "I ain't heard cursing like that since my grandaddy was alive. She's a throwback to the seventies, child."

"I feel unclean," I said as I watched the scene before us. "I mean, it's masterful how she puts words and phrases together, but still…it's…disturbing."

The sound of a car pulling up behind us caused us to turn around. Shay parked his car and got out. As he walked toward us, a frown appeared on his face.

"Miss Roseanna?" he said with a concerned look on his face. "You okay?"

Mama looked at him in surprise. She pointed at the woman. "You know her?"

"Yeah, that's Miss Roseanna," Shay said. "She plays spades with my Aunt Cherry sometimes."

"And another thing, you fat fu—" Miss Roseanna started.

"Oh, Lord," Mama said, shaking her head. "If I'm ever in a fight, I want her on my side."

Shay walked around us. "Miss Roseanna? Miss Roseanna?! Calm down!"

She turned her head to him as if she suddenly realized he was there.

"Oh, Shay. Good. You're here. Arrest him," Miss Roseanna said, pointing at Max.

"I…" Shay looked at Max and then back at her. "I can't arrest him for towing your car, Miss Roseanna. That's not illegal."

"Yes, it is!" Miss Roseanna said in a loud voice. "That's my only car! How am I supposed to get around? Arrest him!"

"Miss Roseanna," Shay said in a pleading tone.

"Miss Roseanna, you don't have to worry about him," Mama said, pointing at Max. "He is soon about to get his comeuppance. Trust me. When they say wait on the Lord, they know what they're saying."

"I can't wait for the Lord. I want to personally give him his punishment. Come here, boy," Miss Roseanna said. "What the—?"

"Hey! *Hey!*" Shay shouted and ran to hit the side of the tow truck that was slowly pulling away from the curb and dragging poor Miss Roseanna's car behind it, causing sparks to fly. Shay cursed and ran back to his car.

"He's not really going to try and flee, is he?" I asked, pointing a hand at the truck.

"I think he is," Mama said in disbelief.

"I don't know if it's me, but shouldn't he go faster if he's in a high-speed chase?" Alexandra asked.

"I would say so," Mama said.

We watched as Max drove down the street at ten miles an hour.

"What should we do?" I asked.

"Catch him!" Mama said and took off running.

"What the—?" I said and ran after her. "We're not running after him!"

"Oh, yes, we are!" Mama said. She glanced at us. "How am I ahead of you two, and you're younger than me?"

"Ugh!" I said and pumped my legs harder.

"Hey!" I yelled, waving my arms at Max. "Hey! You! You, stop it!"

"That is not going to work, Cookie!" Alexandra yelled, breathing hard as she ran.

"Then you come up with something!" I said.

I looked at Shay, who was driving at a snail's pace behind Max and looking very annoyed. I waved my hands at him, and he rolled down the passenger window.

"Do something!" I said to him, pointing a hand at the tow truck.

"What do you want me to do? I'm in a high-speed, slow-speed chase. I've already called for other officers," Shay said. He stuck his head out of the window and yelled, "Max, pull this thing over and stop playin'!"

"Oh, now you want to get loud?!" I said.

"Cookie, stop focusing on me and focus on pumping those legs," Shay said.

"You should have arrested him the moment you saw him!" I yelled.

"*For what?!* Because you and your Mama have a *theory*?" Shay asked in disbelief. "No!"

"Next time, will you trust us!"

"Next time, I'm having you two arrested," Shay said.

"For what?!"

"For bad judgment and not minding your business," Shay said. "There has to be a law on the books for you two—"

Boom!

I jerked back as the tow truck came to an abrupt stop, and Shay stomped on his brakes. Alexandra walked back to me, smiling. I looked at the tow truck; the front window cracked, a large spiderweb slowly spreading across the glass.

"I used to play softball as a kid," she said.

Mama flew past us in the car and screeched to a halt in front of Max, blocking him from driving forward. She got out of the car and walked over to us.

"Are y'all okay?" she asked.

I looked behind me and then at her. "Weren't you running with us?"

"God, no," Mama said, shaking her head. "My hip started hurting. Running is a young woman's game. I don't have time for that. Not in these shoes."

"So, you made me and Alexandra run, but you went back to the car, and…you know what? Never mind," I said with a shake of my head. "It really doesn't matter."

Mama turned, and we watched as Shay pulled Max from the truck to arrest him. Officers flooded the scene, and soon people were standing outside to watch the spectacle.

"Well, girls, we did it," Mama said proudly, a huge smile spreading across her face. "Another case solved by the Simmons' Detective Agency."

*****

"Two murders, high-speed chases, and catching two killers? Wow, Mama, I have to give it to you," Marques said, plopping another spoonful of banana pudding onto his plate. "Only you and Cookie could ruin Easter."

"*Ruin!*" Mama said, turning in her seat to look at him in outrage. "We are the heroes of this Easter story!"

"Isn't Easter about the Lord's sacrifice?" James asked, looking at her.

"Okay, besides that," Mama said, tapping a hand on the kitchen counter. "Me and Cookie saved everyone!"

"And me," Alexandra said, sliding up next to Ren. "I was an integral part of the team."

"Yes, you were," Mama said, smiling at her. "We couldn't have done it without you."

"Yes, you could have," Ren said. "You didn't have to drag poor Alexandra into y'all's mess."

"Mmm, I don't know, Ren. I kind of liked it. Maybe when I retire, I'll open my own detective agency," Alexandra said, smiling up at him.

"God, no," Ren said and shuddered in mock horror.

"The point is that we helped two people," Mama said. "Faith and Khalil are out of jail, Jessica and Max are in jail where they belong, and my ham from Easter is still delicious."

"Oh, my God, you told me it was a new ham!" Marques said, his fork clattering to his plate.

"*There is nothing wrong with that ham!*"

"*I ate six slices, Mama!*"

I shook my head as I ignored the argument between Mama and Marques and got up to answer the door.

"Hey," I said to Shay and stepped back to let him in.

He frowned at all the fussing and leaned down to whisper, "What's going on?"

"Death ham," I said.

"Death ham?" he said. He shook his head in wonder as he closed the door. "Death ham and icees. What is it with you people and food?"

"Company is here! Ya'll can stop shaming yourselves!" I announced.

Everyone turned to Shay and greeted him.

"Hi, honey, you want some banana pudding?" Mama offered.

"I'll take a bit," Shay said, looking at it in appreciation. "Thanks."

I scooped him up some and handed him the bowl and a fork. He took it and nodded his head in thanks.

"So, what are you doing here?" Mama asked.

"I wanted to stop by and tell you that Max turned on Jessica and confessed to everything," he said. He took a bite and hummed in pleasure.

"He did?" I asked in surprise. "What made him do that?"

"I think the thought of going down for two murders when Jessica was the one who planned it caused him to rethink things," Shay said.

"Did he explain why he killed Gary?" I asked.

"Yeah," Shay said, sighing hard. "He panicked. Gary did call Max to ask him if he would go with him to Faith and William's house to tow their cars. Gary came out of the house and complained about Faith wanting paperwork. Max got down with him, and they went into the house. Ashley called Gary to see where he was and if he was coming to their parents' house. Gary was trying to brush her off, but Ashley said something about needing to tell him something important about the bed and breakfast when he got to their parents' house. Max panicked and thought that she was going to tell him that William had come over. He grabbed a knife, stabbed Gary, wiped the handle with his shirt, and left before Faith came down the stairs. He accidentally knocked over Gary's bottle of cranberry juice in the truck, and it spilled all over him and the passenger seat. Jessica took his work shirt and hid it at her place with the idea that she would get rid of it later."

"Had William talked to Ashley?" Mama asked.

"Not according to Ashley, but Jessica didn't know if he had or not," Shay said. "Ashley was in the house, cleaning the bedrooms, and William had come by the house to speak to her, but I guess she didn't hear him when he called out for her. He walked around the house looking for her but couldn't find her. Jessica caught him in one of the bedrooms, and he confronted her about what she was doing and how it was causing people to think that he was a bad businessman. She lied and said Ashley wasn't there, and he left. Jessica tried to talk to Ashley, but she was evasive and edgy, which scared Jessica, and she called Max."

"So, Ashley never saw William?" I asked.

"No," Shay said, shaking his head. "I talked to her. She never knew he came to the house, and she only wanted to talk to Gary about their parents losing their house. Not about William being innocent of cheating her."

"Hmmm, what a shame," Mama said. "All this because of greed."

"Yeah," I said softly and brushed away invisible crumbs off the counter. I looked at Shay. "Is Ashley keeping the bed and breakfast?"

"I think so," Shay said. "Or at least it seems that way. Allen and Ashley said they didn't want to make any rash decisions now that the truth had been revealed. They needed to take some time to think things over."

"Well, that's good," Mama said. "I hope they keep the bed and breakfast. It really is a beautiful spot."

Mama looked at me. "Speaking of beautiful spots, you remember your cousin Chante?"

"I don't have a cousin named Chante," I said.

"She was your play cousin when y'all were kids," Mama said.

"Chante…Chante Jackson?" I asked. "Chante Jackson, who pushed me off a slide when we were six because her 'boyfriend' gave me his honeybun at lunch? *That* Chante Jackson? I still have the scar on my knee!"

"Yeah," Mama said, smiling. "God, she was an awful child. Anyway, she's getting married and needs help with the bouquets. I told her that you and I would come by and help them put them together. It'll be fun."

My mouth hung open.

"No, you did not volunteer me for *another thing!*" I snapped.

"What's wrong with putting bouquets together?" Mama asked.

"Nothin', but the last time you volunteered me led to two bodies and my thighs chaffing because I had to run down a street after a tow truck!"

"You're overreacting," she said.

"Mama," I warned.

"They're expecting us tomorrow at six," Mama said. She turned to Shay. "So, Shay, how is your Aunt Cherry doing?"

I growled and closed my eyes to calm down.

I hate being volunteered for something I don't want to do.

www.ingramcontent.com/pod-product-compliance
Lightning Source LLC
Chambersburg PA
CBHW050325160726
48002CB00001B/190